"It's after twelve midnight," Elliot shouted into the phone. "That means that the apartment now belongs to me. Do I come up there right away and discuss this amicably, or do I storm the place—cops, marshals, you-name-it!—in the morning?"

Paula's jaw tightened. "I have a gun," she said. "I have a gun and I'll use it if I have to."

She slammed down the phone.

"You have a gun, Mom?" Lucy whispered in surprise. "I didn't know you have a gun."

"If you believed it," Paula said, "maybe he will."

She went into the kitchen and opened the refrigerator for a glass of milk. Lucy appeared in the doorway.

"We're in trouble, right?"

"We're not in trouble," said Paula. "We have our rights. Possession is nine-tenths of the law."

"What's the other tenth?" said Lucy.

Paula drank deeply from her glass. "Shut up."

After two minutes had passed the phone rang. Paula looked at it without moving. It rang again.

"Is that the last tenth?" said Lucy.

THE GOODBYE GIRL

A Novelization by
ROBERT GROSSBACH

Based on the Original
Screenplay by
NEIL SIMON

WARNER BOOKS

A Warner Communications Company

WARNER BOOKS EDITION

Copyright © 1977 by Neil Simon
All rights reserved

ISBN 0-446-89556-3

Warner Books, Inc., 75 Rockefeller Plaza, New York, N.Y. 10019

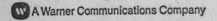 A Warner Communications Company

Printed in the United States of America

Not associated with Warner Press, Inc. of Anderson, Indiana

First Printing: November, 1977

10 9 8 7 6 5 4 3 2 1

THE GOODBYE GIRL

Chapter 1

It was, for her, a flash of total, rotten insight, "a moment of cosmic consciousness," as the Rosicrucians called it. One instant, as she and Lucy entered the apartment, she was singing Tony's name in a weird falsetto voice, her head filled with thoughts of dinner and the shirt she'd bought him and the trip —and then, in the next, her eye had caught the envelope. Wedged under the selector knob of the television set, Channel 5 pointing to the finicky, precise lettering. "Paula." And she knew in that terrible, plummeting, sinking second that it was all over, again, *again*, and that her future would be filled with dried tears, and bitterness, and lonely, aching frustration.

The day had started on an upbeat—bright sun (although later it began to cloud up), clean, crisp air, a feel of fast-paced, brisk, New York City action. They'd hit Macy's and Korvettes early, then walked over to Lexington Avenue where they'd taken the IRT to 59th Street. For some reason, there was no sense of incipient tiredness, only a boundless, spunky energy. From Bloomingdale's they crossed to Alexander's, where they waited for twenty minutes in the children's shoe department until a squat, Latin-looking salesman finally called their number.

"I goh a fi'ty chwan."

"That's us, Ma," whispered Lucy urgently.

Paula yelled out, "Here!"

The salesman came over, smiling. "Jes?"

"We'd like to see something in a sneaker," said Paula. "For the young lady, here."

"Sonthin' in a snikker," echoed the salesman. "You chab anythin' particular in mind?"

"We have a sneaker in mind," said Lucy. "Two of them, in fact."

"Bu' you chab to say chwa kine of snikker. You chab to say 'Pumas.' Or, 'Adidas.' Or, 'Keds.' Or sonthin' like tha'."

"What's the cheapest?" asked Paula.

"All the same."

"What's the difference between them?"

"All the same."

"Then just pick a random sneaker."

The salesman cocked his squat, brown head. "Chwas 'Random'? We don' chab 'Random'."

"I can't take much more of this," said Paula.

"Me neither," said the salesman. "Thas chwhy I goin' on vacation next week. I go back where I come from."

"Oh," said Paula, trying to be polite. "How nice. Very nice. We're going on a trip next week, too."

She and Lucy both looked at each other and smiled conspiratorially.

"Hey!" said the salesman jovially, "Thas son coincidence, hah? Is tha' the chway you say? 'Co-incidence'?"

"Yes. Perfect."

"Good. I measure you up now, young miss. Then

8

I go see if we goh 'Random' in your size. Otherwise, I bring you Keds, jes?"

Lucy nodded, and the salesman removed her shoe and measured her foot. When he'd gone, Lucy said, "Is that man Spanish?"

"Mmm, Puerto Rican, I would guess," said Paula knowledgeably.

Later, when they had paid for the sneakers, Paula called to the salesman on the way out. "Have a nice time in Puerto Rico," she said.

"Puerto Rico?" said the salesman. "Chwhose goin' to Puerto Rico? I come from Jackson Heights."

Her name was Paula McFadden and she was a mature-looking thirty-three. *Willowy* was the word for her. Tall, tight-hipped; not "great" legs or "gorgeous," but "good" ones; small, hard tush; minimal tits; a shade too much lipstick; nice unspectacular hair. And a face with character, a face with a veneer of toughness not quite sufficient to mask the underlying hurt.

Crossing 59th Street, she said to Lucy, "C'mon, we'll go in someplace for a snack. Whaddaya want?"

Lucy looked up, her small hand cradled in Paula's. "You know what I'd like?"

"What?"

"What I'm really in the mood for?"

"Wha-at?"

"Moo Shoo Pork."

"Oh no." They reached the other side of the street. "Oh, no. None of your crazy foods now. Oh no. Why can't you want normal foods like other ten-year-old girls? No Moo Shoo Pork now."

"All right," said Lucy, resignedly. "Ice cream, then."

9

"That's better," said Paula.

In the luncheonette, they sat in a small booth and ate sundaes—chocolate fudge for Paula, butterscotch for Lucy.

"This time next week," said Paula. "California!" She looked at Lucy. "You excited?"

"Uh-huh."

"Me, too. Can't wait."

"Were you ever there?" asked Lucy.

"Once," said Paula. "For six weeks. Touring with some musical. Middle of December, we went swimming. It was so war—"

"Which musical?"

"What?"

"Which musical were you in?"

"What's the difference? I'm trying to tell you how beautiful it's going to be. We're going to look for a little house up in the hills. No smog . . . sunshine every day . . ."

"Near the movie studios?" said Lucy.

Paula felt very much like hugging her.

"Yes. Near the movie studios. Your window will face Warner Brothers. You can watch them blow up the world from your bed, all right?" She let the image of a house drift into her mind. Bay windows, country kitchen, stone patio, huge garden with . . . "Can you imagine having your own orange tree and lemons and—"

"I think the musical was *Fiddler on the Roof.* I remember. I think I was staying with Grandma. Wasn't I around four and a half?"

She made horrible, high-pitched scraping noises with her spoon on the bottom of the sundae glass.

Why did she always seem to concentrate on off-center points, thought Paula. "Stop that!" she said aloud. "And no, you were never four and a half.

10

Personally, I think you're a forty-year-old midget masquerading as a kid."

"Don't call me a kid," said Lucy. "Kid means goat."

"Sorry," said Paula. "I meant child."

"If you really want to apologize you can get me a take-out order of Moo Shoo Pork."

Paula smiled and shook her head no.

"Then how about a dem sem?"

"No!"

She used to tell people that she lived "just off Central Park West," but actually it was a lot off Central Park West, and the neighborhood was generally referred to in newspaper accounts as "decaying." The principal location advantage was the fact that they were within walking distance of the Museum of Natural History and the Hayden Planetarium, although after the first ten visits, this had seemed like progressively less of an attraction. Paula felt that it was certainly *nice* that Lucy knew the names of all the dinosaurs and their geological epochs, but it was hard to make the link between that and anything that could improve your lifestyle.

They walked slowly past the rundown brownstones, and the potholes and fire escapes—tired finally, but not really rundown, anticipating supper and a second wind. They passed a large puddle.

"You see that?" said Lucy. "You see that puddle?"

"Yeah."

"You see how you can see colors in it?"

"Yes."

"What makes those colors?"

Paula shook her head. "Baby, you know science

11

was never my strong point. Why don't you ask Tony when we get up?"

"Ohh." Lucy groaned. "He won't know, either. He never knows things like that."

They walked on, finally coming to the entrance of their building. Paula stopped by the mailboxes to check if anything was there. Nothing. They began to climb the stairs, holding the rickety, decrepit wooden bannister and pushing one foot after the next. On each landing were profuse and detailed graffiti, pictures of women copulating with men, copulating with horses, with chickens, with discombobulate genitalia, with celery, with wood. . . . And then there were the advertisements: "For a Good Lay call Paco, 831-5741," "For the time of your life, Julius —355-1892." And finally, the advisories: "Spanish Avengers smell like shit," "I suck young girls," etc. Paula always felt terribly embarrassed passing the signs, not for herself (actually, they were rather interesting) but for Lucy, with whom she never discussed them, or mentioned them in any way.

They passed the third floor, Mr. Horvath's floor, the lisping Hungarian with a predilection for overalls, who always left a piece of liver on some tinfoil outside his door, and as a result had a congregation of cats that honored him with a chorus of meows whenever he entered or left. They trudged on, finally making it to the fourth landing, where Paula took out her keys.

"Can I show Tony all my things first?" said Lucy.

"Later," said Paula. "You've got homework to do."

"Why?" said Lucy. "We're moving in four days. Why should I do my homework?"

"Suppose between now and Friday they teach brain surgery. I don't want you to miss it."

"We did that already," said Lucy, brightly. "Last week. In science. We did it."

Paula stopped walking. "You——. Come on, are you serious?"

Lucy looked at her. "Ma! Jesus, Ma, you're so dumb. How could you——? Ma!"

"Well, I don't know," said Paula, defensively. "I thought maybe in frog dissection. . . . What do *I* know?"

They entered the apartment. It was a small, three-room affair with a tiny vestibule that led into a living-dining area off which were a kitchen and two dinky bedrooms. Show posters from *Steambath* and *The Indian Wants the Bronx* were Scotch-taped to the wall above the couch, and several theatrical photos of Tony were placed strategically around the room. The coloring of the plaster had originally been beige, but time and cheap paint had combined to lead the way into a kind of dismal, welfare-type khaki.

"Can I just show him my blue sweater?" said Lucy, when they'd put down their packages. "And the new jeans?"

"All right," said Paula. "But brush your hair and wash your face."

Lucy took her things and started for her room.

"And no makeup!" yelled Paula.

She crossed the living area, slowly opened the door of her bedroom, and peeked inside. The bedding was mussed and disarrayed as usual. She entered.

"Tony? Oh, To-oh-oh-neeeee." She put down the packages. "Hey! You in the bathroom? Hey, we cleaned out Korvettes." She began to open the box with his shirt in it and peeled away the layers of tape. "We bought everything on sale, so you'd better like it 'cause we can't exchange it." She removed the shirt, a sport shirt, picture of Rodin's *The Thinker* on the back. "Hey, we bought you a present! Come on out and take a look. Tony?"

She crossed the floor and knocked gingerly at the bathroom door. "Tony? You. . . ." She pushed the door open. Empty. She went back in the living room. On the mantel the photographs stood in stern array—Tony DeForrest, actor, full-front; Tony, profile; Tony and Paula; Paula and Lucy . . . Then Paula's gaze fixed on the TV.

In her room, Lucy had just pulled down her sweater when she thought she discerned a scraping sound. Or was it a whimper? She was buttoning up her new jeans when suddenly she heard something with absolutely no ambiguity: a scream. Her mother's scream, a wail, really, a shriek that tapered into a moan of absolute, utter despair. Lucy rushed out, her heart beating frantically.

In the center of the living room, Paula stood holding a letter, the tears running down her cheeks and over her lips.

"What ha—? Ma! Ma! What happened?"

Paula turned to her full-face.

"He's gone. He left without us."

Chapter 2

Lucy fought to assimilate the information. "You mean Tony? Tony left for California without us?"

"For Italy," Paula sobbed.

"Hah?"

Paula sat down heavily in a chair. The letter hung limply in her hand. Lucy gently pried it loose.

"Can I read it?"

Paula sobbed and seemed not to hear as Lucy began softly reading the letter aloud.

" 'Dear Paula. This isn't an easy letter to write.' It doesn't start off too good, does it?"

Paula began choking and waving her hands. Lucy, unnoticing, continued.

" 'Where the hell do I begin? You know you and the kid mean a lot to me.' The kid, he calls me. 'I turned down the job in L.A. It was just a lousy TV picture any—' "

Paula had finished choking. "Must you?" she said tearfully.

"Must I what?"

"Read it out loud?"

"Ma, I don't like to read to myself. I'll say it very low."

Paula began to cry again.

" '. . . anyway. On Monday Stan Fields called. I got the Barto . . . Barto . . . luk—' "

"Bartolucci."

" '. . . Bartolucci picture.' Who's Bartolucci?"

"An Italian director."

"What'd he direct?"

"What do I know?" said Paula. "What are you asking questions like that now for?"

Lucy shrugged and continued. " 'It's six months shooting in Spain and Italy. It's a hell of a part, Paula, and I want it. I broke my ass—' "

Paula snapped up. "All right, never mind now. Give it to me." She held out her hand.

"Ass!" said Lucy. "So what? Ass. I heard the word."

Paula thought of the hall graffiti and realized that ass was nothing by comparison.

" 'I broke my ass for twelve years in this town and things are finally beginning to break for me. I told you when you first moved in here with me that it was never going to be permanent. I remember, I told you that. Christ, I'm not even divorced yet from Patti.' Who's Patti?"

"I told you about her."

"No, you didn't."

"I thought you would be upset if you were living with a married man," said Paula.

"*I* wasn't living with him," said Lucy. "*You* were. I was in the next room."

"Well, they were *practically* divorced."

Lucy returned to the letter. " 'I left early today because I didn't think a goodbye scene would do any of us any good!' This is one of the worst letters I ever read in my whole life."

"It's terrible," said Paula. "Terrible, terrible letter."

" 'I wish I had something to leave you and the kid.' He didn't leave us anything? Not even one thing?"

Paula shook her head no.

" 'You know I've been in hock up to my ears. I had to sell my watch and my camera to pay off the loan sharks.' What's a loan shark? How could he owe money to a shark?"

"I'll tell you some other time," said Paula.

" 'But I know you'll be all right. You can always go back to dancing. You—' "

"You hear that?" interrupted Paula. "You can always go back to dancing. Dancing! I'm thirty-three. I can hardly walk any more. Let *him* go back to dancing."

" 'You deserve more than I can give you. I wish the both of us all the luck in the world. Love to the kid.' "

"Don't read any more," said Paula. Then, in a hoarse voice, "Please."

"It's just a little more."

"Lucy, please."

"Just one more word." She looked down. " 'Tony.' "

She placed the letter on the side of the couch. Paula put her arm around her. "Does this mean we're not going to California?" asked Lucy.

Paula nodded. The tears began to come again.

"That means I have to do my homework, doesn't it?"

Paula nodded again and cradled Lucy in her arms.

Neither of them could sleep. At eleven-thirty in the evening, Paula entered the kitchen and found

17

Lucy seated at the table, alone, staring up at the ceiling.

"You neither?" said Paula.

Lucy shook her head.

Paula held out her arms, and Lucy rose from the chair and cuddled into them. The tragedy for Lucy was a good deal more specific than it was for her mother: she was not going to California. While there was substantial concern for Paula's well-being, there was very little for her own, and even less for Tony's. Lucy had the child's implicit confidence in the eternal existence of her body and the jaded adult's reluctance to form lasting emotional attachments. She'd always sensed something in Tony that prevented her from getting close to him, and now that the situation had erupted, she was surprised, but not *that* surprised. She was, after all, more so than Paula, in touch with her subconscious, which had always recognized the possibility.

She stroked her mother's hair. "How about some sardines?"

"What?" said Paula.

"A snack."

Paula laughed and hugged her tighter. "How come you like all these peculiar foods, huh?"

Lucy shrugged, and Paula continued chuckling.

"How come you're laughing?"

"Me? I donno. I'm laughing at us. At me. I'm so dumb, it's hysterical."

"Weird sense of humor."

"You'd think I would've learned my lesson," said Paula. "Married an actor, and he walks out on me. Lived with an actor, and he flies out. Next time I talk to an actor, kick me in the . . . you know the word."

18

"Ass," said Lucy. Then, with mock brightness, "Hey! Why don't we go to California anyway? Maybe you can get into television. *Everybody* gets into television."

"We haven't got enough money to get through the Lincoln Tunnel," said Paula.

"We can sell the furniture."

"It belongs to the landlord."

"Mr. Spielman?"

"The little angel himself."

"We can sell it late at night," said Lucy. She took a strand of hair and put it in her mouth.

"I think Tony's left his mark on you," said Paula. "Look, don't worry, I'll get a job. I can still dance. I just have to get back into shape. I can do it."

"I know."

"But you're worried."

"No."

"Tell me."

"I told you."

"I mean, tell me what you're thinking about now."

"Well," said Lucy, "I was wondering about how you can owe money to sharks."

Paula turned away. "I'm sorry," she said, "that's not the kind of thing I can deal with right now."

The jokes were not jokes. You could *smell* them a mile off. There were twenty-two of them, in black leotards (like Paula), in white, in bathing suits, in gray sweatsuits, even gym shorts (one of the men). They were a mixed group, a few professional dancers, some actors, housewives, businessmen, and others of no clear occupation. In condition they ranged from the sleek, muscled, practicing pros who just came for a quick workout, to the flabby East 70s matron who thought this would be

changed her mind after three stabb

Paula stood near the back line, gr

strain of keeping up with the instruct

who was counting off the exercises.

"Bend . . . bend . . . bend, hep,
arch, and . . . arch, and . . . back,
I see you, Paula." Musically. "Paula
can't hide from me."

I'm going to kill her, thought Pa

"And . . . toes, two, three, four.
four, My God, Paula, what have
body?"

"It died," said Paula, stoppin
respect."

She sank exhausted to the floo

A half-hour later she was dresse
at a soft drink vending machin
quarter, pressed the button for
Nothing happened. She pressed a
pushed the coin return button an
the little compartment. Nothing.

"Shit!" she said aloud.

A voice behind her said, "Pa

She turned quickly and fou
blankly at a young woman of
brownish-blondish hair.

"Hi," said the woman. "Do
the swing girl when you were i

"Oh," said Paula. "Oh, yeah.
her forehead. "Whew!"

"Tough getting back into sha

"It's been two years. It's am
get when you're happy."

A man came over, put a quar

20

"Ass," said Lucy. Then, with mock brightness, "Hey! Why don't we go to California anyway? Maybe you can get into television. *Everybody* gets into television."

"We haven't got enough money to get through the Lincoln Tunnel," said Paula.

"We can sell the furniture."

"It belongs to the landlord."

"Mr. Spielman?"

"The little angel himself."

"We can sell it late at night," said Lucy. She took a strand of hair and put it in her mouth.

"I think Tony's left his mark on you," said Paula. "Look, don't worry, I'll get a job. I can still dance. I just have to get back into shape. I can do it."

"I know."

"But you're worried."

"No."

"Tell me."

"I told you."

"I mean, tell me what you're thinking about now."

"Well," said Lucy, "I was wondering about how you can owe money to sharks."

Paula turned away. "I'm sorry," she said, "that's not the kind of thing I can deal with right now."

The jokes were not jokes. You could *smell* them a mile off. There were twenty-two of them, in black leotards (like Paula), in white, in bathing suits, in gray sweatsuits, even gym shorts (one of the men). They were a mixed group, a few professional dancers, some actors, housewives, businessmen, and others of no clear occupation. In condition they ranged from the sleek, muscled, practicing pros who just came for a quick workout, to the flabby East 70s matron who thought this would be a good idea, but changed her mind after three stabbing chest pains. Paula stood near the back line, grunting with the strain of keeping up with the instructor, Miss Marian, who was counting off the exercises.

"Bend . . . bend . . . bend, hep, three, four . . . arch, and . . . arch, and . . . back, two, three, four. I see you, Paula." Musically. "Paula. Oh, Paula. You can't hide from me."

I'm going to kill her, thought Paula.

"And . . . toes, two, three, four. Toes, two, three, four, My God, Paula, what have you done to your body?"

"It died," said Paula, stopping. "Have a little respect."

She sank exhausted to the floor.

A half-hour later she was dressed and staring down at a soft drink vending machine. She inserted a quarter, pressed the button for *TAB*, and waited. Nothing happened. She pressed again. Nothing. She pushed the coin return button and fished around in the little compartment. Nothing.

"Shit!" she said aloud.

A voice behind her said, "Paula?"

She turned quickly and found herself staring blankly at a young woman of medium height and brownish-blondish hair.

"Hi," said the woman. "Donna Douglas. I was the swing girl when you were in *Company*."

"Oh," said Paula. "Oh, yeah. Sure. Hi." She wiped her forehead. "Whew!"

"Tough getting back into shape, isn't it?"

"It's been two years. It's amazing how flabby you get when you're happy."

A man came over, put a quarter into the machine,

20

pressed the button for *TAB*, and got his drink in the opening below.

"You know I lived with Bobby," said Donna.

"Bobby who?" said Paula.

"*Bobby. Your* Bobby."

A sudden flood of memories cascaded through Paula's consciousness. Her Bobby. Bobby Kulik. Beautiful, beautiful Bobby, with the dimple in his chin and the twinkle in his eye. And no change in his pocket. The one she'd fallen madly, totally, head-long in love with. The one she'd dreamed about and thought about and got so excited over that she'd *squirmed* during the day just imagining being with him at night. The one with plans and lofty aspirations and tender, touching hopes and childish yearnings. The one she'd married and dedicated herself to completely. Who'd fathered Lucy. That one. The actor. Bobby the bum, who'd left her screwed, blued, and tattooed. Who'd run out when the impulse got too much for him. Poor Bobby.

"Oh," said Paula now. "Oh, *that* Donna. You know I just didn't make the connection before. How is Bobby?"

"Beats me," said Donna. "We split three weeks ago. He's living with my ex-roommate now. They *both* owe me money."

Paula laughed cynically as Donna put a quarter in the drink machine. A *TAB* came out as soon as she pressed the button. "Forget it," said Paula. "If he hasn't paid me, he's not gonna pay you." A sudden heat stabbed up the length of her back and made her wince. "Hey, do they do spine transplants?"

Donna sipped her soda. "I heard you and Tony are moving to California. That's wonderful, really wonderful. Listen"—she lowered her voice—"I'll tell you something, you're well rid of Bobby."

"I'm well rid of Tony, too," said Paula with a brightness she didn't feel. "He moved out last night."

Donna stopped sipping. "Oh, jeez. Oh, Paula, I'm—. Jesus . . . actors."

"Tell me about 'em!" said Paula.

Donna excused herself then, explaining she had to catch another class. Paula felt a network of tiny threads begin to form a million knots of pain throughout her body. She reached over and pushed the *TAB* button, waited an instant to verify that nothing happened, then resignedly inserted another quarter into the slot. Again, the button. Nothing. "Why?" she said aloud. An elderly woman nearby looked at her.

Paula took two steps away from the machine, then abruptly whirled and kicked it on the side. "Ahh!" She groaned in pain.

"Dehumanization," said the old woman. "That's the principal product of this society."

Paula stared at her dully, then walked out the door and down the flight of rickety stairs to the street. She did not see the old lady cross confidently to the machine, press the button, and gleefully lift out her *TAB*.

She stopped in at Finast to pick up some groceries, buying a few of Lucy's favorites, then headed down along 78th Street until she reached her building. She walked with great stiffness and imagined herself half submerged in a steaming, fragrant tub of deliciously hot water. It was the only thing that kept her going. She paused for a moment as she reached the steps of her brownstone, and just as she did so,

22

Mrs. Crosby emerged from her basement apartment. Mrs. Crosby was a large, tough, independent black woman who had been appointed by the landlord as "manageress" of the building. Mrs. Crosby regarded the tenants as holding positions somewhere between employees and prisoners.

"You leavin' tonight or in the mornin'?" she asked Paula now.

"I'm sorry," said Paula, her mind full of soap-suds and warm, wet total body immersion. "What was that, Mrs. Crosby?"

"Just checkin' on what time you vacatin'."

"Oh. Oh, well, we're not going to California. I forgot to tell you."

Mrs. Crosby looked undisturbed. She regarded Paula from shrewd, porcine eyes. "Well, I ain't th' only one you forgot to tell. That apartment been sublet."

"What?" said Paula, trying desperately to snap out of her fog. "What are you talking about? We're paid up through July. We've got three more months. You can't sublet that apartment."

Mrs. Crosby stared at her. "*I* didn't. Your man did, honey."

Paula whimpered involuntarily, a small, scared, animal sound. "He . . . sublet . . . our . . . apartment?"

"Tol' me las' night," said Mrs. Crosby in her best police witness tone. "See, it was his name on the lease, so he can do what he wants."

"But—"

"Clause three C, honey, 'Should the lessee desire to sublet said premises before expiration of this contract, he must notify lessor not less than—'"

"All right, all right."

"You jus' be sure you leave it the way you foun' it. Don' you go takin' no—"

"I'm not leaving it!" screamed Paula, furious. "*I* cleaned it, and *I* painted it, and *I* decorated it, and it's *mine. Me.* I don't care what he did, I'm not getting out, you understand?" She was somewhat shocked by her own outburst, but also glad it had happened before she could issue a recall.

Mrs. Crosby remained unflappable. She'd dealt, after all, with a lot worse than this. "Tha's none of my business, honey. You can take that up with the suble*ttee.* I jus' don' wan' no trouble in my building, tha's all." She started back toward her apartment.

Paula just stood there. Presently, she began screaming. "That bastard! That no-good, son-of-a-bitch bastard!"

"Uh-huh!" agreed Mrs. Crosby as she disappeared behind her door.

The pictures of Tony DeForrest sailed through the heavy night air, the vicious, pouring rain soaking the cardboard backings even before they hit the pavement, where the protective, non-glare glass cracked in jagged segments and scattered along the wet concrete. Paula stood at the window, not quite sane, and flung the pictures out into the nighttime storm, one by one. On impulse, she turned and sent a particular photo hurtling against an interior wall, badly chipping the plaster and denting the picture's frame. Lucy walked in carrying a tray with a dish of sardines, two glasses of milk, and some Mallomars. She looked at the picture on the floor.

"And you're always telling me to clean up *my* room!"

"Come on," said Paula, "let's take those into the bedroom."

24

"I thought you said eating in bed brings roaches."

"The crumbs. The crumbs bring roaches. We'll eat without crumbs. Come on. We'll have a crumbless snack."

She shut the window and, as an afterthought, shuddered against the previous chill. She followed Lucy into the bedroom. She stripped quickly, leaving her skirt, blouse, bra, and stockings in a heap on the floor, slipped into an old, torn nightgown, and slid under the covers next to Lucy. She reached for a glass of milk that Lucy had put on the night table and drank it down about halfway.

"Did you brush your teeth?" she asked. The head of a sardine was disappearing in Lucy's mouth.

"Uh-huh."

"Did you?"

"Yes."

"C'mon, did you really?"

"I did! Ma, I did."

"The lady doth protest too much, I fear. All right, you did. I hope so. Because the way things are going, we aren't about to spend a hundred dollars at the dentist's right now. If you get a cavity, you'll just have to adjust to it."

"I'll adjust to it." Lucy stared at the foot of the bed. "How'd you do in dance class today?"

"I got winded putting on my leotards," said Paula. She took another sip of milk. "You upset by all this?"

"No."

Paula reached over and cradled Lucy's face in her hands. "Of course you are. Are you?"

Lucy tried to answer, but Paula's palm was under her jaw. "A li'il," she finally got out.

"Look," said Paula, "we're gonna be all right. You trust your mother?"

25

"A li'il," said Lucy.

"A girl in dance class told me there's a musical auditioning tomorrow. I'm gonna go down. I think I've got a fair chance." She removed her hands from Lucy's face.

"Good," said Lucy. "Then you'd better watch your diet. How 'bout giving me your cookies?"

"Oh, listen," said Paula, "you already—"

The doorbell rang, and they both jumped.

"What's that?" said Lucy, involuntarily cuddling closer to Paula.

"You don't know what that is?" said Paula.

"I know what it is," said Lucy, "but *what . . . is . . . it*?"

"I don't know," said Paula. She switched on another light. A childish part of her mind said: Maybe if I ignore this, it will go away. She looked at the clock. "Who rings the bell at such a time?"

"Hey," said Lucy, sitting up. "Maybe it's Tony Maybe he changed his mind and came back."

"You're so young," said Paula, who'd almost, but not quite had the same thought.

The bell rang again, longer this time, and more insistently. Paula got out of bed and put on an old bathrobe.

"Stay here," she said.

"If you're not back in an hour," said Lucy, "I'll call the sheriff."

Paula walked through the darkened living room. As she approached the door, the bell rang again.

"Who is it?" she said irritably, aiming her voice at the doorknob.

There was no answer from the other side.

"Who is it?" said Paula again.

26

There was a pause. "Is there a Tony DeForrest there?" asked a male voice.

Paula didn't answer.

"Because I'm supposed to sublet his apartment."

Chapter 3

Elliot felt like shit. He'd gotten off at the Port Authority Bus Terminal after eleven o'clock, having ridden a Greyhound for twenty-five hours coming in from Chicago. As usual, he'd searched the bus for good-looking chicks he could sit next to, and as usual, he'd ended up near a sailor from Baltimore who was fixated on Johnny Unitas.

"Ah don't keer how much this kid Jones scores, there's no one gonna tell me he got it up here like Johnny U," the sailor had commented. He was pointing to his forehead, and the remark was the first thing he'd said to Elliot.

Elliot, a kind of vague sports fan but certainly no student of any game, had nodded agreement.

"Johnny U knew how to use his fullback. You gonna tell me Jones knows how to use a fullback?"

"No," said Elliot. "No, I wouldn't tell you that."

"Who was he?"

"Who?"

"Johnny Unitas's fullback. Bet you don't even know."

Jeee-sus, thought Elliot. Why couldn't I be next to some runaway debutante with psychiatric problems or something? We could work out her manic-depressions between here and Cleveland, and from there to New York it would be all mufkee-pufkee. He extended his hand to the sailor.

"Elliot Garfield," he said. "And I'm afraid I really don't know much about football. Gale Sayers and Billy Wade on the old Bears, and that's about it."

The sailor slowly took his hand and began pumping it. "Well," he said. "Reuben Brand's the name here, goin' to Baltimore, an' at least you got the guts to admit when you don't know somethin'."

Elliot smiled, gave a little wave, and opened his book on the philosophy of Spinoza. He turned on the little overhead spotlight and tried to focus his eyes. Outside, it was dusk, and the pinpoint city lights were just beginning to come on, fending off the blackness of the encroaching night. The tires hummed on the pavement as Elliot slid down in his seat. He felt peculiarly chilly, and he hunched his coat tightly about him, trying to get the material to rest against his face. It was a chill born not of actual cold, but rather of loneliness, and fear, and excitement. True, he was going to New York, and he had an opportunity there, and things were looking up, but there had been no one to see him off at the bus terminal, neither family nor friend, and now he was alone. He felt detached, isolated, a drifter going through the motions. He dipped into the Spinoza.

Surely human affairs would be far happier if the power in men to be silent were the same as that to speak. But experience more than sufficiently teaches that men govern nothing with more difficulty than their tongues.

"What're you, a lawyer or somethin'?"

The voice intruded on Elliot's consciousness and he looked up. "Huh?"

The sailor had taken off his hat. He was a big

29

kid, with a long, twisted nose, and Elliot could see now the deep V-shaped intrusions in his hairline. Baldness. The kid was homely, and now he was going bald.

"I'm sorry," said Elliot. "I was trying to read."

"I jus' wanted to know if you were a lawyer, is all," said the sailor. "I mean I seen you readin' the book there."

"Oh. Oh, no. Not a lawyer. Actor, I'm an actor." Elliot looked down.

"A actor? You? Holy cow. Ya know, I kin'a thought you might be somebody. A actor! Holy—. Hey, did I ever hear of you? What's your name?"

"I think I told you before," said Elliot. "Elliot Garfield."

The sailor nodded profusely and turned the name over and over in his mind. "Elliot Garfield, Elliot Garfield, Elliot, Elli—" He looked up. "Hey! Wasn't you once on *Kojack*?"

Elliot shook his head. "No." He tried to return to Spinoza.

Nothing exists from whose nature some effect does not follow.

"Got it!" said the sailor suddenly, after nearly twenty minutes had passed. "Got who you are. I knew I seen you someplace. You was in that war picture. M*A*S*H. With them nurses. Hee-hee. That was some goddamn movie."

Elliot shook his head. "That was Elliot Gould," he said. "He's a different person." He took off his black-framed glasses and smoothed out his beard. It was going to be a long ride.

It wasn't until after their first ten-minute stop at a Howard Johnson's that the sailor finally asked, "Okay, what movies *was* you in?"

"Reuben," said Elliot, "I don't do movies, or at

30

least I haven't yet. I haven't done TV, either. I'm a play actor. I do Shakespeare, Shaw, Pinter, Albee . . . plays."

Reuben nodded silently. "I never seen a play. I don't think they got plays in Baltimore—'cept football plays, o' course, heh—an' I *know* they ain't got plays in Seattle."

"That where you coming from, Seattle?"

"Yup. Got mahself three weeks. Three weeks ta do nothin' in."

"Lots of luck," said Elliot. "I hope you accomplish your purpose."

Once, after the third stop, he'd been tempted to change seats, especially when a thin girl with a big chest encased in an orange sweater sat down two rows ahead. But an odd sense of loyalty had intruded, a feeling that he'd be rejecting Reuben in some way, and he'd held his ground. Spinoza was the only philosopher he could begin to understand, and he read his book with a mixture of pleasure and grim determination. He could never figure out whether he really liked it, or whether he was reading it simply because he felt he should. His father had read Spinoza, seemingly with much more ease as well as understanding, and Elliot had often puzzled over how such an unintellectual man could be so comfortable with the most profound ideas and concepts. Like so many other facets of his father, this one would remain an enigma that ended in the grave—the postal clerk who liked Spinoza.

It may easily come to pass that a vain man may bec—

"How old are you?"

"What?"

"How old are you?" said Reuben.

"Say, Reuben, uh, I'm trying to read something

31

here which is very difficult for me. Lemme just finish this, and I'll be right with you."

"Maybe I can help ya. I read pretty good. What's the part you're havin' trouble with?"

Elliot pointed to where he'd left off. "It's not exactly trouble, it's just. . . ."

Reuben's eyes moved slowly over the passage.

. . . *become proud and imagine himself pleasing to all when he is in reality a universal nuisance.*

Elliott waited many seconds before Reuben looked up. Empty, black countryside spilled by outside. Dim shadows, trees, shadow-shapes of houses, rolled up, passed, were gone. There's really nothing out there, thought Elliot. Nothing.

"Says somethin' 'bout a nuisance," said Reuben, finally. "That help you any? Nuisance?"

"Yes," said Elliot. "Thank you. I'm thirty-four, by the way. And it's not that I don't want to do movies. I do, believe me. I just haven't had the chance, that's all."

"I'm eighteen," said Reuben brightly.

"That's nice," said Elliot. "Very nice. I wish I could be eighteen again."

He knew, try as he might, that he would never be able to speak to Reuben without patronizing him. Hours later they slipped across the border of New York State, and hours after that they entered Manhattan, where the rain came pouring down in buckets. Elliot grabbed his duffel bag and guitar case as they got off the bus. He turned to Reuben as they waited for the driver to open up the baggage compartment.

"Listen, uh, if you got some time, I'll buy you a beer, huh? Whaddaya say?"

"Oh," said Reuben, smiling. "Well, that's real nice of you to offer, Elliot, but I gotta catch a connecting bus for Baltimore, supposed to leave

32

in ten minutes, 'cording ta my watch. What time you have?"

Elliot searched the walls, found a clock. "Eleven-thirteen," he said. "I think we're a little late."

"These shit-eaters are always late," said Reuben. "Thanks, anyway."

Elliot picked up his suitcase from where the baggage handlers had set it, and extended his palm to Reuben. "Luck, sailor."

"You, too," said Reuben. "Hope you make it to *Kojack*."

Elliot began walking away. When he was nearly to the staircase, he heard a "Hey!" and turned quickly around.

"Alan-the-horse-Ameche!" yelled Reuben.

"What?"

"Unitas's fullback."

Elliot waved his hand in thanks and disappeared quickly up the exit steps.

Twenty minutes later, he was getting out of a cab on West 78th Street. He handed the driver three dollars, said, "Keep the change," and ran for the door of the old brownstone. He chugged quickly up the steps, hauling his baggage behind him. When he got inside he paused to wipe his glasses, which were covered with water. He knew the frames would soon break into blotches. That's what happened with cheap plastic frames; expose them to water and apparently they absorbed some of it and become temporarily discolored. The effect, for the one or two days it lasted, was really quite bizarre. He removed a corner of his shirt from inside his pants, and carefully cleaned the lenses before replacing his spectacles. He started up the steps, banging his bag and guitar randomly into the walls and bannister each time he made a turn. He read the obscenities on the walls and smiled. Good stuff. Finally, he got to the fourth floor, pulled his belongings up after him to the landing, and walked over to the door. His glasses had misted over again. He pulled the key from his coat pocket, inserted it in the lock, and turned. He rotated the doorknob and pushed. No good. The door was bolted shut.

He rang the bell and waited. Waited.

He rang again. Waited.

A woman's voice answered finally, annoyed.

"This is Elliot Garfield," said Elliot. "Is Tony in?"

"There's no Tony here."

"What?" Funny, but with his glasses fogged, he also seemed to have trouble hearing.

"There's no Tony here."

"There isn't? Tony DeForrest?"

"There's no one by that name here."

"Wait a second," said Elliot. He fished around in his pocket until he found a small slip of paper, which he withdrew. He removed his glasses and held the paper close to his eyes, checking carefully the address and then the door number before him. "This is the right apartment," he said to the door. "I was here once, about two years ago."

"I don't care what apartment you've got," said the voice on the other side. "There's no Tony De-Forrest here."

"Could you open the door a second?" said Elliot, beginning to lose patience.

"Not twenty-to-twelve, I can't."

"Jesus," said Elliot. "Look, you got a chain there or something. Keep the chain on, and just open it a hair. I just want to talk to you."

There was a pause, and several rustling, clinking-metal noises, and then an inch-wide crack appeared and Paula was peering out.

"Make it fast," she said. "My husband is sleeping."

Elliot felt like groaning. "Listen, there's gotta be some mistake. I just sublet this apartment from this friend of mine. Tony DeForrest. He lives here."

"That'll be news to my husband, Charlie," said Paula in her best wise-guy tone.

"Look," said Elliot, fishing ineptly in his coat again. "I got a receipt in my pocket for three months' rent. I sent him a check. I was supposed to move in tomorrow, but I came in early because I start work in the morning, and I thought I could spend the night here. You look a little confused. Uh . . . can I speak to your husband?"

Elliot put his glasses back on.

"He'll be at the thirty-seventh precinct," said Paula, quickly. "Nine o'clock in the morning. Just ask for Charlie D'Agostino. Homicide. Good night."

She slammed the door.

Elliott, dazed, dripped all over the landing.

Inside, Paula took a deep breath. Please, she thought, please go away. Even if it's just for tonight, then go away for this one night. She walked back to the bedroom and took off her robe. She climbed into the bed with its incredibly sagging mattress. "You could take anyone," Paula had once told a friend, "Muhammad Ali, Bruce Jenner, anyone, someone in top physical shape—he sleeps here one night, guaranteed he wakes up a cripple." She rolled over near Lucy.

"Who was that?" asked Lucy.

"Never mind," said Paula.

"It didn't sound like 'never mind' to me."

"Tony rented the apartment," said Paula. "To

someone. But I'm not giving it up. It's ours. Go to sleep."

Lucy turned over, her back to Paula. Then she twisted around again. "He rented the apartment?"

Paula nodded.

"What a shitheel!"

The rain streamed down and soaked through his hair and beard. His bags hung limply from his body. On the sidewalk, Elliot stood and tottered uncertainly. This was really ridiculous, he thought. Really ridiculous. That woman. Something wasn't kosher about—. For a brief instant, a quarter of one of his lenses cleared enough to see through. His eye caught a sign. *Manageress*. What the hell is that? He walked closer, but a *splat*! of water from the stoop closed off his vision and he staggered down the few steps to the door of the apartment below. He rang the bell. And waited. Presently, a voice said, "Who there?"

"Hello?" said Elliot. "Are you the super? Hello? Listen, my name is Elliot Garfield and I just subleased an apartment upstairs, but there's someone in there who won't let me in."

"What you say?"

Elliot began to raise his voice, but realized that with the driving rain and howling wind as competition, there was no hope. "Listen. Could you open the door a second?" he yelled.

"Ah ain' openin' no do', so you may as well say whatevah it is you got to say."

"Are you the super?" yelled Elliot.

"Ah is the manager," said Mrs. Crosby.

"Well, I'm getting soaked here," yelled Elliot. "I subleased an apartment upstairs. You hear? Subleased. Me. But they won't let me in. Can you hear? Hello?"

"Yeah."

"They won't. . . ." His voice trailed off. It was hopeless.

"You got a problem," said Mrs. Crosby, "that between you and the lessee. Ain' no concern of the lessor. An' tha's all I'm sayin'."

Elliot had already climbed the steps and grabbed up his luggage. He trudged down the street, a blind, listless animal, soaked to the bone. After two blocks he found a phone booth and squeezed inside. He could hear himself breathe. He removed a slip of paper from his coat pocket, extracted a dime from the change purse of his wallet, and inserted the dime in the phone. There was no dial tone. Elliot pressed up and down on the receiver cradle. Nothing. He pushed the coin return button. Nothing. Elliot began to moan.

He spotted another booth diagonally across the street. *What else is there to try?* he asked himself with surprising reasonableness. The rain drenched him, assaulted him, attached itself to every part of his face and body. He ran across the street, afraid of slipping, afraid of his mind's image of himself sprawled in the gutter, the cars heedlessly splashing past, his luggage strewn in abandoned disarray. He made it to the other side and wedged himself into a new booth. He inserted a dime in the phone. *Please. Please.* He got a dial tone, and slowly, with extreme, accountant-type caution, he began to dial.

Lucy had begun to dream. She was in school, only the school was in a cave, and every twenty minutes or so a huge, moving shadow appeared at the cave entrance, and Mrs. Murdoch, the teacher, would pause in the middle of a sentence and her features would become distorted with fear. There were only about eight or ten students in the class, and Lucy had begun to weasel her way toward the rear of the cave when— *Brrrinnnng!*

Loud. Go away. *Brrrrinnnng!*

Insistent.

Rrrrrinnnng!

Lucy awoke and sat up. "It's not for me," she said to Paula, who'd also arisen. "All my friends are sleeping."

"Shut up," said Paula.

The phone rang again, and Paula lifted the receiver.

"Hello?" said Elliot into the mouthpiece. "Hello, is Tony there, please?"

"Who's calling?" said Paula.

"You *know* who's calling," said Elliot. "I was just up there. I recognize your voice, Mrs. D'Agostino."

"Mrs. Who?" said Paula, then—too late—remembered.

"D'Agostino!" said Elliot, leaning heavily against the walls of the booth. "And how come your telephone answers to Tony DeForrest's number? And how come the key he sent me Air Mail Special Delivery opens your door? Hah? *Hah?* You want to answer those questions, Mrs. D'Agostino?"

"No," said Paula. "Why don't you answer them?"

"All right," said Elliot. "I will." In the distance, two men walked slowly up the street. "The answer is something fishy's going on up there. I'm wet as a herring, Mrs. Whatever-your-name-is. I don't have a place to sleep tonight, and I don't want to blow my last few bucks on a hotel." He looked at his watch, a water-resistant model. It had stopped at ten after twelve. The two men he'd seen in the distance were now approaching the booth. Slowly. What kind of a person, thought Elliot, walks slowly in this weather?

"According to my waterproof Swiss watch," he continued, "it's . . . uh . . . it's after twelve, which means that apartment technically belongs to me. Now, do I come up there right now and discuss this amicably, or do I storm the place—cops, marshals, you-name-it—in the morning?"

Paula's jaw tightened. "I have a gun," she said. "I have a gun, and I'll use it if I have to."

Elliot instinctively jerked the receiver from his ear as she slammed down the phone.

The two men were right outside his booth, standing next to his luggage. The big one in the longshoreman's jacket and woollen cap kicked absently at his duffel bag. The other, dressed in a business suit, grinned at him. Elliot wanted to withdraw his wallet to look for more change . . . but thought better of it. There were not many viable options. He opened the door of the booth as the big man stepped back.

"Some rain," Elliot said pleasantly, stooping to pick up his guitar.

"Hey, buddy," said the longshoreman, forcefully. "You got any change?"

This is it, thought Elliot. They're going to kill me. Actor, just in from Chicago, slain on West 76th Street. No, no. Unemployed actor. No. Unidentified man. That's it. Unidentified man *found* slain. Perfect.

"Hey!" repeated the big man. He seemed oblivious to the rain. "Hey, I'm askin' ya. You got any change?"

The question had no right answer. "No" was inflammatory. "Yes" meant he'd have to withdraw his wallet, after which they would rip it from his

39

grasp and knife/garrote/stomp him into unconsciousness.

"I think I only have bills," said Elliot. "I need some, too. Wait a second."

He stepped out into the street and waved his hand. Two cars flashed past, a cab, another car.

"Change!" he yelled, pulling out his wallet and extracting a dollar bill. He waved the bill in the rain. "Hey, change! Change of a dollar!" The cars continued to whiz past. "Hey, pregnant wife in the lobby, I need change!"

A taxi screeched to a halt, and Elliot ran to it. He considered getting in, and just getting away, but looked back at his luggage and abandoned the idea. *He died for his guitar.* "Change of a dollar," he said breathlessly to the cabbie. He proffered a limp, sopping-wet bill. "It's an emergency."

The cabbie looked out at him. "Tell you what, bub. I'll give you fifty cents. Take it or leave it."

"Jes—all right. Okay. Here."

The cabbie handed out the coins, then rolled up the window. Elliot walked back to the curb and over to the big man. He held out the coins. "I can only give you twenty cents," he said. "The bastard driver would only give me fifty."

A dim hope burned that perhaps the man would see this as an act of camaraderie, he and Elliot joined in common cause against gouging off-duty cabbies. The longshoreman removed one dime and two nickels.

"He's a little under the weather," he said, turning to prop up his associate in the suit. "I need to call someone to pick him up."

The thinner man looked up and spoke in a thick, determined accent. "I happen to be chief engineer

40

of a small but technologically advanced Long Island company."

"That's . . . very nice," said Elliot. And then, facing the big man, "Go ahead, you can go first. He looks in bad shape."

"No, no," said the big man. "The rain's good for him. The water rinses him off. You go."

Reluctantly, Elliot nodded and squeezed back into the booth. The two men outside stared at him. Elliot fed his first dime into the slot.

"You have a gun?" said Lucy. "I didn't know you have a gun."

"If you believed it," said Paula, "maybe he will."

Paula went into the kitchen and opened the refrigerator. She poured herself a glass of milk. Lucy appeared in the doorway.

"We're in trouble, right?"

"We're not in trouble," said Paula. "We have our rights. Possession is nine-tenths of the law."

"What's the other tenth?" said Lucy.

Paula drank deeply from her glass. "Shut up."

After two minutes had passed the phone rang. Paula looked at it without moving. It rang again.

"Is that the last tenth?" said Lucy.

"Go back to bed," said Paula. "I'll handle this."

"Hello?"

"I just called the thirty-seventh precinct," said Elliot. "There *is* no Charles D'Agostino in homicide! Then I called Rita Scott, an old friend of mine. Rita Scott is an actress who was in *Merchant of Venice* in the park this year with the ever-popular Tony DeForrest. Rita also told me all about this girl Tony's been living with for the last twelve months. A certain Paula McFadden, a former dancer, and

41

her ten-year-old daughter, Lucy. Rita further told me that the apartment—"

Outside, the big man was examining Elliot's guitar case.

"—the apartment in question is leased in the name of Tony DeForrest. She knows this for a fact because Rita used to live with Tony, the smoothy, prior to Paula and Lucy."

Elliot paused to breathe.

"Now then, can we continue this conversation in a drier room, Miss McFadden?"

The answer came back instantly. "You got problems, take it up with the Housing Authority. Goodb—"

"Wait! Wait. Don't hang up! Please, don't hang up. I don't have any more change. I'm soaked to the bone, Miss McFadden, and I have a very low threshold for disease. I don't know what Tony told you, but he's got my money, I have a lease, and you've got the apartment. Now one of us got screwed . . . uh, let me rephrase that. We have to talk this out. I'm in no condition, financial or healthwise, to look for a hotel in the pouring rain. If there's such a thing as the Seventy-eighth Street strain of swine flu, I think I've got it."

He remembered going in with a friend to take the flu shots and waiting on a long line for the hand-injected vaccine (supposedly the "gun" was worse) and finally getting to the area and seeing the signs. *Report any symptoms of dizziness, breath shortness, retching, vomiting, or foaming at the mouth.* "That's it," he'd told his friend, leaving the line, "I could take all the others, but the foaming did it. No foaming things for me."

"Why don't you take a shot in a convenient place?" said Paula.

Outside his glass enclosure, Elliot saw the two men begin to walk away. They were laughing.

"Five minutes," said Elliot, "that's all I ask. Look, in about thirty seconds we're gonna get cut off, Miss McFadden. My number is"—he removed his glasses and squinted at the phone—"eight-seven-three, five-two-six-one. It's a flooded booth on West End Avenue. If you have any compassion in your heart—"

"Five cents for the next three minutes" came the voice of the operator.

"I'm trying to work it out, operator," said Elliot, his voice rising. And then, to Paula, "If you have any human compassion in your heart, you'll call me back. The number again is eight-seven-three, five-two-six-one. That's eight-seven-thr—"

The phone clicked off. "Ah, shit!"

With a sinking feeling, Elliot fished around in the coin return box. Nothing. He blew on his fingers, then wrapped his arms tightly around himself. He felt his knees beginning to buckle. *Assume fetal position . . . Now!* A police car slowly cruised by, the cops looking balefully at Elliot's booth.

He waited. Presently, he pulled himself up and pushed open the folding door. The rain was still heavy, but the wind had let up just a bit. He grabbed his duffel bag and slung it over his shoulder, took his suitcase in one hand and guitar in the other. He began to lurch uncertainly down the street. When he'd taken three steps, the phone rang.

Chapter 4

Elliot leaned heavily on the doorbell. He was exhausted. He looked as if he'd just been immersed in a pool. He wiped his glasses on a corner of his shirt as he waited. After a moment, the lock turned, the chain clinked off, and the door opened.

"Thank you," he said gratefully.

"Five minutes!" said Paula.

Elliot stooped to pick up his luggage.

"Leave your bags," said Paula. "This isn't a permanent conversation."

He nodded and walked in. Paula closed the door. Inside, Elliot wiped his forehead with a soaking wet handkerchief.

"I'm dripping on your rug."

"It's been dripped on before," said Paula.

She walked into the living room and stood near the false fireplace, one arm on the mantel. All right, she thought, so he wasn't dangerous. But he was annoying. And persistent. And his purpose—she mustn't forget—was to evict her and her daughter from *her* apartment. It would be a cold day in July before she'd let *that* happen.

"Look," said Elliot, "I'm sorry about all this.

44

I really am. I didn't know there were going to be any complications."

"Yeah, well," said Paula, "there's a lot of that going around lately."

"Okay," said Elliot, beginning just now to look her over, "I don't blame you for being hostile. I get the picture. Tony rents me the apartment, splits with the money, and you and your daughter get dumped on. Right?"

"That's your version," said Paula. *Remember, concede nothing. Not one inch.* "My version is that Tony and I amicably ended our relationship, we agreed I would keep the apartment, and you and your six hundred dollars got dumped on. Get the picture?"

Elliot grinned in spite of himself. He nodded. "Very good. Nice. Very sharp. A sharp New York girl, right?"

"No," said Paula. "A dull Cincinnati kid. But you get dumped on enough, you start to develop an edge."

Elliot thought: Under other circumstances I might actually enjoy this. The woman seemed a bit of a shrew, but she wasn't bad to look at, and there was something, a certain softness, that might even be appealing. Still, he needed to sleep tonight.

"Okay," he said, "so what's the deal? I have a lease in my pocket. You gonna honor it or not?"

"I got a daughter in my bed," said Paula. "That tops a lease in your pocket."

"Look," said Elliot. "C'mon, I don't want to get legal. Legal is on my side. I happen to have a lawyer acquaintance downtown. Now all I have to do is call this downtown lawyer acquaintance of mine and—"

She was smiling.

45

"Oh, Jesus!" she said.

"Huh?"

"An actor!" Paula said.

"What?"

"Another goddamn actor! 'I happen to have a lawyer acquaintance.' That's right out of"—she was shaking her head—"*Streetcar Named Desire.* Stanley Kowalski in summer stock, right?"

"Wrong!" said Elliot, irate. "I played it in Chicago in the dead of winter. Three and a half months at the Drury Lane."

Paula waggled her head from side to side. "Ask an actor a question, he gives you his credits."

"You want the reviews, too? said Elliot. "Here: 'Elliot Garfield brings new dimensions to Kowalski that even Brando hadn't investigated.' Okay?"

Paula pursed her lips. She began to look more closely at his face, trying to penetrate the beard. Not unattractive, really, sort of a short, furry, caricature of Paul Newman. Or almost. Similar cocky manner.

"Terrific," said Paula. You have a terrific imagination. You write beautifully. Aren't you a little short to play Stanley?"

"No one noticed," said Elliot. "I stood on the poker table. What are you, a critic?"

"No, no," said Paula. "I love actors. As long as they stay up on the stage where they belong. Put 'em down in real life, and the whole world gets screwed up."

"I don't think you're really being fair to—"

"Well, I've had enough, I really have. I'm not getting kicked out of the same lousy apartment twice. You want your money back? Hah?"

"Well . . . yeah, if—"

"Then go to Naples. You want this apartment?"

46

Elliot didn't answer.

"Then buy me two tickets to California." Paula was rolling now. "I'll give you two minutes to think it over before I yell 'Rape!' "

Elliot was shaking his head. Strangely, the longer he stood there and the worse things she said to him, the more appealing she seemed to get. Mama bird defending her nest against all odds.

"Jesus," he said. "You are *something*. It's a wonder Tony didn't take a job in the Philippines."

"I hope you're thinking," said Paula, "because I'm counting."

"Wait a minute!" said Elliot. "Wait a minute, willya? What if we made a deal?"

"What kind of deal?" Paula asked warily.

"I don't know," said Elliot, stalling. *How about I just pass out unconscious on your floor, right now? That's a deal I could deliver on.* "Let me think of one. I just got here. Could I have a cup of coffee?"

"No." *Donate an inch, he'll roll up a mile.*

"Don't be bashful," said Elliot. "Just say what's on your mind. All right, look, here's the situation—"

"I *know* the situation."

Elliot clicked his tongue. "Would you do me the courtesy of at least hearing me out? Hah? Would you do me that? You're not the only one who can yell 'Rape!' you know. All right. We're in a bind here."

"Clever analysis, Holmes."

"*The both of us*," continued Elliot. He swallowed, and spoke rapidly. "And I think the only practical solution is to share this apartment."

"I accept," said Paula.

"What?" Elliot could not believe the information

47

his ears had just accumulated. He thought he was hallucinating.

"I accept," repeated Paula primly. The decision had been intuitive and instantaneous. "I may be stubborn, but I'm not stupid."

"You mean it?"

"I have a daughter who goes to school, and I have to start looking for a job. You have a key. I'd have to stand guard all day to keep you out."

"You have a chain lock," said Elliot.

"Those crumble if you talk too loud," said Paula. "You could be in in a second."

"You could add additional locks." What am I doing? thought Elliot. Trying to wreck my own case?

"Anything I'd add or put on, I'd have to give Mrs. Crosby a spare key. With your signed copy of the sublease, she'd have to give you a duplicate."

"You could call the cops," said Elliot.

"So could you," said Paula with finality. "No, you win. Get your bags. You get the small bedroom."

He looked at her, nonplussed, as she headed for Lucy's bedroom. He started out to the hall. What the hell was he getting himself into here? He opened the door, picked up his luggage, and brought it inside. He closed the lock, feeling a kind of wicked irony in the action. He looked around the living room, spotted a picture apparently dropped on the floor, and walked over to pick it up. It was Tony. *One of those "friends" who saved you the effort of acquiring enemies.* He lifted it tentatively to the mantel, then changed his mind and replaced it, face down, on the floor.

"Where are you?" he said aloud.

"I said *the small bedroom*!" came Paula's voice.

48

Elliot crossed the living room and opened the door—to the wrong room. The light was on, and Lucy was sitting up in bed staring at him.

"Oh," said Elliot. "Sorry. Guess I have the wrong room. I'm Elliot."

"Hello," said Lucy, bewildered.

"You must be Lucy."

"That's right."

"I'm Elliot Garfield. I'm moving in the other room."

"Oh?"

"I'm a friend of Tony's."

Lucy glared at him. "That's nice."

"I'm an actor, too."

"Oh, yeah?"

"Your mother knows," said Elliot.

Lucy seemed to be sizing him up. Not entirely favorably, either. "I see."

"So," said Elliot, trying to sound chipper. "I guess I'll be seeing you around."

Lucy said nothing.

"I'll see ya," said Elliot.

"I guess so."

"Well . . . good night." He closed the door. From inside he heard the word, "Jesus!"

He crossed the living room and opened the door to the other bedroom. On the bed Paula had piled an immense array of shirts, blouses, jeans, sweaters, socks, slips, panties, furry toy animals, magazines, and records.

"I just met Lucy," said Elliot.

Paula was kneeling in one of the closets. She looked up. "What did you tell her?"

"That I was moving in. She seemed to take it in stride."

Paula ducked down again and came up with a

49

handful of shoes and torn sneakers. "You grow up fast in this apartment. Look—" She thrust her face forward, pointing with her chin. "The john is in there." She rose from the closet and walked over to the bed. She picked up the entire enormous pile of clothing and junk and began to move toward the door. A Beachboys album fell off the top.

Elliot rushed to retrieve it and placed it back on the pile.

"I'll get the rest of her things in the morning," said Paula. She moved into the little hall outside the bathroom.

"Hey!" said Elliot.

She looked around.

"Hey, listen, you think you can stop grinding your teeth for two minutes? The noise is driving me crazy."

Paula glared at him. "Look, a stranger from Chicago with a wet beard and dirty sneakers moves into my daughter's room, and you expect smiles? Forget it."

Elliot was conscious of the water squishing between his socks and the bottom of his sneakers. It reminded him of his high school years when he'd worked for Mr. Nimkoff, the druggist, and had to make deliveries in wet weather—people could hear him coming hundreds of feet away. *Shhwish, shhwish.* His feet were still bad from that job. Its only advantage, in fact, was that occasionally Nimkoff let him work behind the counter where he could steal a few prophylactics and learn which neighborhood women used which intimate products. He looked at Paula and grinned.

"Hey, you know, you're dynamite! I love listening to you talk. I hate . . . *living* with you, but the conversation is first-class."

He waited for the effect of his praise. Waited for the sudden softening, the dewy-eyedness that was so easy to bring forth in women. Women. Even when they knew you were bullshitting them and flattering them, they still ate it right up. *That's a lovely dress you're wearing today. That's terrific perfume you have on. Your hair really looks gorgeous.* Women. Unbelievable.

"This is *your* room," said Paula harshly.

"Huh?"

"*Your* room," she repeated. "I don't clean or make beds. You can use the bathroom or the kitchen when I'm not in it—and wash up when you're through."

This broad sounds like my mother when I was eight years old, thought Elliot.

"You pay for your own food," continued Paula, "your own laundry, linens, and phone calls. I'd appreciate some quiet between six and nine every night because that's when Lucy does her homework."

Elliot had widened his eyes and was nodding in exaggerated parody of obsequiousness. "Anything else?" he asked.

"Yes. I don't care what you drink or smoke as long as it's not grass in front of my ten-year-old daughter. Now, do we have everything straight?"

Elliot had begun to dislike her again. This woman was all venom. Cold as a snake.

"You forgot to tell me I can't eat candy between meals," he said, "or go outside in the rain without my rubbers—which, incidentally, I could've used—or to show you what I did in the bathroom after I've finished. Oh, and the answer to your question is: No, everything is not straight."

Paula cocked her head. "No?"

"I'm sorry, but I'm not crazy about the arrangement."

"You're not?" Paula felt her false bravado begin to slip away.

"Definitely not," said Elliot. *Time to show this bitch who's boss.* "I'm paying the rent, I'll make the rules."

Paula nodded in a simulation of Elliot's previous mannerism, but couldn't quite achieve the same unconcerned, faintly bemused effect. Difference between a dancer and an actor, she thought. The word "actor" braced her a little. He might be bluffing down to his shoes, but his theatrical training was helping him put up a front.

"I take showers every morning," continued Elliot loudly, "so don't have your little panties drying on the rods."

Actually, he'd once lived with a girl who'd had that habit, and it really didn't bother him at all at the beginning. In fact, it was somewhat erotic, seeing them there in the mornings, and in the shower he'd sing songs to them, to their individual parts. Hello, elastic waistband, he'd bellow as the warm spray of water woke up his body. I love you, reinforced cotton crotch. But gradually, as the months passed, the girl, a clerk in a dry-cleaning shop, had become moody and depressed and begun to consume huge quantities of food. The bikinis over the tub had gradually become hip-huggers, and then the huggers had become regulation briefs. When the briefs had escalated into loose-fitting trunks, Elliot had fled the shower, and that had been the end of the relationship.

"I like to cook," continued Elliot, "so I'll use the kitchen whenever I damn please. And I'm very careful about my condim—"

A look of shock came over Paula's face.

"*Condiments*," said Elliot. "Condiments. So keep your salt and pepper to yourself." He paused, thinking for a moment. "I play the guitar in the middle of the night when I can't sleep, and I meditate first thing in the morning. Complete with chanting and burning incense, by the way, so if you gotta move around, let's have a little tiptoeing."

He was getting to her. He could see it in her face, see the mouth open ever so slightly, the gaze begin to drop. He thought about his meditation. Years ago, he'd been going through a period of intense, nervous unhappiness, questioning the entire value of his life, his work, his motives. Then one day he'd gotten a call from Howie Dennis, an old friend he hadn't heard from for years. He'd invited Dennis over for dinner and had been quite surprised when his old friend appeared in toga-like clothing.

"Jesus, Howie," he'd said, "is that the way they dress at IBM?" The last he'd heard, his friend was working at the computer giant after having taken courses in programming.

"Oh, I'm not with them any more," Howie had said. "I work for the Maharishi Institute."

"What?"

"They operate out of Switzerland."

"Switzerland? What do you do in Switzerland?"

"Oh, I don't work in Switzerland. They send me all over the world—Saudi Arabia, Tanzania, Nepal, everywhere—and I set up computers for people and program them. It's all on a contract basis. 'Course I send the money I'm paid to the Institute, and I keep just enough to live on."

Elliot had shaken his head, trying to fit his friend into this new, stretched framework of existence.

53

"C'mon, I have dinner," he'd said.

"I'm vegetarian," apologized Howie. "Sorry. Don't worry, though. I brought my own stuff."

He'd then produced a bag of dried fruits and nuts and other plant-like consumables, and had eaten them sparingly, while Elliot had gorged on the roast beef. After dinner, Howie had persuaded him to try Transcendental Meditation.

"I just—" said Elliot, "I mean, the little man with the high voice, the Indian who operates out of Switzerland? I mean, it's such an obvious ripoff. . . ."

"I've been doing it for two years," said Howie, "and it's worked wonders. I'm happier now than I've ever been. I'm divorced, I'm free, and most of all, I'm at peace with myself."

Elliot had nodded reluctantly. "Well, I'm at war with myself."

"Try it," Howie had said. "Cost you ninety or a hundred bucks, and it might just work. It really has a strong scientific basis, and if it fails—well, so you're out the hundred. If it's a success, though, it's worth millions."

"You're pretty persuasive," said Elliot.

"It's because I believe it. By the way, could you loan me a ten, till Thursday?"

Elliot had loaned him the ten, and had gone the next week to a TM center, where he'd listened to a lecture, been introduced to an instructor, and been given a *mantra* to repeat during his periods of meditation. "Twenty minutes in the morning, twenty minutes at night," the instructor had said. "Think of absolutely nothing. Let your consciousness come up as bubbles rise in a pond."

Elliot had tried it for two weeks, then reported back. "I can't seem to get any bubbles."

He'd kept at it, though, at first often falling asleep

during the meditation periods, but gradually, gradually finding himself less keyed up, less uncertain, more relaxed. Apparently, for whatever reason, even if it were only a self-fulfilling belief, there was something to it. He'd been practicing it ever since.

Once, years later, he'd run into Howie. "How's the Maharishi?" Elliot had asked.

"Maharishi?"

"You know—TM, Switzerland?"

"Oh, that. Oh, I don't do that any more. I think it was all a fraud. I'm with the Hazeltine Corporation now. Government Products division."

"You owe me a ten," Elliot had commented.

His mind snapped suddenly back to the present.

"Also, I sleep in the nude," he told Paula.

Her gaze flicked up.

"With the windows open, summer, winter, rain, or snow. I also may have to go to the can or to the fridge late at night, and I don't feel like putting on jammies, which I don't own in the first place. So—"

Her jaw dropped. He had her.

"—unless you're looking for a quick thrill or your daughter wants an advanced education, I'd keep my door closed."

She'd begun to nod again.

"Those are *my* rules and regulations," said Elliot. "How does *that* grab you?"

"And if I say no?" said Paula, looking directly at him.

She had nice, big eyes. Elliot began to like her again, just a tiny bit.

"I have this lawyer acquaintaince—"

"I accept," she said.

"Hey!" said Elliot. "Now, we're movin' right along."

55

"Look," said Paula. "I don't like it, and I don't think I like you."

She'd said *think*, recorded Elliot. That was a qualifier. "Why—because I'm an actor?"

"Because of that, and also because you have the personality of a walrus. That's mainly it, your personality."

"It's probably why we were thrown together," said Elliot. He was too tired to be jaunty. "One of God's little jests. Now if you'll move your shapely little fanny out of my room, I'll unpack and dry my beard."

Paula raised one hand to close the door.

Elliot smiled, too broadly. "Miss McFadden."

She stopped.

"You forgot to say good night."

"I was working," said Paula, "on goodbye."

She slammed the door, hard.

In her room, Paula dumped the pile of things on a chair and took off her robe.

"You have my Jim Backus record?" Lucy asked anxiously. "I hope you have my Jim Backus record."

"What?"

"It's a forty-five. You have it?"

"Lucy, I took everything."

"Yeah, but I don't see it."

"Lucy, if you had it there, I got it here. Leave me alone already."

Lucy studied her. "How long is he gonna stay?"

"As long as he lets us," said Paula, climbing into bed. "You have to go to the bathroom? Go to the bathroom!"

"I don't have to go now."

"Then save it till the morning. It's not safe out there." She turned so that her back faced Lucy.

"No kiss?" said Lucy.

"I'm angry," said Paula. "And I want to stay that way. I don't want to lose it. We're gonna need it."

She pulled the covers up around her head. After about a minute, she pulled them down again. "Well, if *you* don't have to make, I do!" She got out of bed, put on her robe, opened the door, and walked out. She found herself tiptoeing. In the bathroom, she was acutely conscious of the tinkling sounds in the toilet, the splashing that came from her. Was he listening, too? The fiend. Pervert. Probably listening at the door. She found herself holding back, trying to minimize the flow. When she'd finished, the flushing sounded like a crash of cymbals, the water running in the sink like a burst hydrant. The fiend! She was living with a maniac. She tiptoed back to her room, closed the door, and slipped into bed. She leaned over and kissed Lucy on the cheek.

"Good night, baby."

"Good night," said Lucy.

Paula felt a tiny bit better. She faced the other way and tried to fall asleep. The thoughts kept intruding: *Sure, get to sleep. Your life has collapsed, but you pay it no mind. You go to sleep.* All right, I won't sleep, came the answer. She was paying for her sins, that was the only explanation. She'd been wild when she was younger, had fooled around with boys, cut classes, barely escaped high school, and in general had never lived up to her mother's expectations. This was the natural result. Cause and effect. Cut chemistry, and you'll end up abandoned and rooming with bearded perverts. A natural law of the universe. Poor Paula. It was really very simple. She was who she was, and that was that. Schoolwork had never interested her. At age thirteen she discovered that sixteen-year-old boys were more exciting than elementary algebra. By fourteen, she was smoking two packs a day; at sixteen, she lost her virginity on a Sunday afternoon to a menacing, heavy-set City College boy named Lenny.

"I love you, Paula," he said in the small, red-lit side room of the dingy fraternity house. "You get me crazy, you know?"

"I know, but Lenny—"

"I gotta have it, Paula."

"Len, look, I like you, but—"

He was on top of her, bulky, heavy-breathing, pressing her down. He reached for something in his pants.

"If you don't put out for me, Paula, I'm gonna have to kill ya!"

"Kill me? But you just said you loved me!"

"I do, I do. You know I'm insane about you, but —you better let me take these off, Paula!"

She felt his heavy ham hands pulling on her underpants. "Lenny!"

He pushed hard against the side of her face, very hard, twisting her neck and partially suffocating her in the pillows of the couch. "Okay," she said, muffled.

He let her up, and she quickly gulped in air.

"Okay," she said. "Just take it easy, will ya!"

"I love you Paula," said Lenny, when he entered her.

The pain had fortunately been minimal; so, of course, had been the pleasure. But there was some, some feeling there, and it was easy to imagine that with the right guy it could be. . . .

She had many boyfriends. Many. She made it out of high school by the wisp of an eyelash and persuaded her mother that she wanted to be a dancer.

"Ma, I can't go to college. I'm not college material. You can't see that? I'm not college material."

"What's that mean, 'college material'? What is that—like wool? Nylon? What's that mean?"

"It means I have no head for studying, Ma. I can't work in an office, either. Look, if I go to Sharry Williams's school they promise to set you up with a certain number of auditions. It's something I know I could do, Ma. I like dancing. I've always liked it."

"It's not a career."

"It is a career."

"Who tells you that? Those bums you run around with?"

"They're not bums. Ma, I'm sorry. I'm sorry I'm not the daughter you constructed in your head. But I'm not, so what should I do? I'm not cut out to be a doctor, or a lawyer or a business woman. I'm just not."

"Then be a nun."

"Ma—"

"Why, it's so bad to be a nun? At least you're looked after the rest of your life. And I'll tell you something, you'd redeem yourself a little in your father's eyes."

"That would require me to be a saint," said Paula. "A nun isn't near enough."

Her mother had looked at her, and then suddenly they were in each other's arms. "My poor baby," her mother had said, the tears cascading down. "You can't help being who you are. It's not your fault."

"It's no one's fault, Ma. No one's."

In the end, her mother had persuaded her father to shell out the money for dancing school, and it had changed Paula's life. She'd quit smoking, gone cold turkey, and done it successfully. The exercise did wonders for her body, making her tight and trim, *toned*, and even, somehow, seemed to lower her sex drive. She had a sense of accomplishment, of achievement. She'd gotten a job on her first audition—a miracle, supposedly—in a revival of *Top Banana*. All right, she missed on seven in a row immediately after that, but she clicked again on the eighth. She began to get some TV work. Not much, but some. She went out with a different type of man, other dancers, a producer once. And then came a job in a new hit show, *L'il Abner*. Broadway. And a minor actor named Bobby Kulick.

Music.

Paula sat bolt upright in bed. Was she dreaming? Had she been asleep? No, she still heard it. Soft music. A guitar.

"*Cchhrrist!*" said Paula out loud.

Lucy stirred and sat up.

"Did that guitar wake you?" asked Paula.

"No. You did."

"I'm sorry."

"Is he gonna play that all night?"

Paula, jaw set, had gotten out of the bed. "Put the pillow over your ears."

"I'll smother."

Paula put on her robe. "It's better than that guitar."

She stormed out of the room.

Elliot's room was dark, except for the dim light of a small night lamp. Elliot was using a quiet arpeggio strum and playing "El Paso." The fingers of his right hand flicked the strings rapidly and clearly, while those of his left came down in sure measured rhythm just in front of the frets. His enlarged silhouette mimicked him on the wall.

An angry knocking intruded itself in the song.

Elliot continued to play, but the knocking got louder, and faster. Still not in time with the music, thought Elliot. He stopped strumming.

"Who is it?" he called musically.

"Very funny," came Paula's voice. "Can I come in?"

"The door's open," said Elliot in lilting tones.

"Are you decent?"

"I am decent."

Paula barged in, furious. "Do you realize it's three o'clock in the morning, and my daughter has to get up at—Jesus Christ, you're naked!" Instantly, she whirled around. "I saw something," she muttered to herself, "but I don't know what I saw." And then, loudly, "I thought you said you were decent."

Elliot was smiling. "I am."

"But . . . you're naked."

"I am decent as well as naked."

"Listen," said Paula, her back still turned. "I have a growing daughter who's not going to grow on two hours of sleep a night."

She was still somewhat flustered by the image of Elliot's nude body. True, the guitar had covered some of it, but she had caught a glimpse . . . and it wasn't bad. "Do you have to play that thing at this hour?" she continued.

Elliot stared at her ass. Or rather at the protrusion in her robe where her ass was contained. He was bemused. This was fun, talking to people's backsides.

"I told you," he said. "It helps me to fall asleep." *Second only to a good piece of ass.*

"Have you ever tried pills?" said Paula acidly.

"I don't know how to play pills."

"It's not hard. You pop them in your mouth and swallow."

61

Elliot sat up straight. "I am a person of health," he said, and punctuated his statement with a short flamenco riff. "I do not put unnatural things in my body."

Ladies and gentlemen, thought Paula, *we have here, right here on our stage, living right next to our own bedroom and sharing our kitchen and bath, one of the world's foremost mental cases. Let's hear it for the maniac, everyone.*

"Music is one of nature's sedatives," said Elliot, strumming softly

"So is a hammer," said Paula.

"If you'll just listen to it instead of fighting it," said Elliot, "we'll all be asleep in five minutes." He began to hum as an accompaniment to his strumming. "If it really bothers you, take two sleeping pills and put one in each ear . . . la da da dee da da dee dummm dum . . . ."

Paula stormed out, slamming the door behind her.

In her own bedroom, she could still hear the guitar. She took off her robe and crawled into bed.

"He won't stop," she said bitterly. "I'm gonna get a lawyer in the morning." She looked over at Lucy. "Just take deep breaths and count to a hundred. I'm sorry, baby. I'm really sorry you got caught in the middle of all this. Lucy?"

She raised herself on one elbow and stretched to peer at her daughter. "Lucy?"

Lucy was fast asleep and snoring.

Paula pulled the blanket over her head and lay on her back. Why do things like this continually happen to me, she thought. Maybe I *should've* been a nun. Better off. She rolled onto her side. Damn guitar. I'll break it. That's what I'll do. When he leaves in the morning, I'll break his guitar. Snip the strings with scissors and . . . . No good. He'll get new strings. I'll have to break the body. Bash it in with something, or. . . . Wait, I can borrow a saw from Mr. Horvath. Paula twisted onto her stomach and buried her face in the pillows. If I was a nun, I'd never have had Lucy. And besides, there—

There was a badly struck twang. And then a second and, very weakly, a third. Paula waited for the strumming to resume. She raised her head. Silence. She strained to hear. Nothing.

"Everybody but me," she said aloud. She dropped back onto the bed and thought of ways to destroy guitars.

She slept.

"Om mommanomma, om mommanomma, om . . . ."

Paula snapped awake. God, she hadn't slept at all! What the hell was—oh, Jesus! Chanting. A chanting sound from the other room. *His* room. The room of the mental case.

"Om mommanomma, om mommanomma, om mommanomma. Om. . . ."

"What's that?" Next to her in the bed, Lucy was sitting up.

"It sounds like God," said Paula, yawning. She glanced at the clock on the end table. Five to six.

"Boy," said Lucy, "does God get up early!"

Om mommanomma, om mommanomma, om mommanomma, om momma. . . .

Lucy sniffed. "I smell strawberries burning."

Paula stood up and put on her robe. "It's incense."

"What's incense?"

"It's what I'm feeling right now."

Paula crossed the room, opened the door, and

walked down the tiny hallway to Elliot's bedroom. Tentatively, she looked inside. Just what she needed to wake up to—a naked man, chanting. He was not in the bedroom. She walked into the living area.

In the middle of the room, on the floor, Elliot sat in the full lotus, or *padmasana* position. In front of him was a small vase with a rose and a burning stick of incense. He wore a sweatsuit and a prayer shawl around his shoulders, and had his eyes closed. As she watched, he placed his hands behind his back, palms together, fingers pointing upward, and slowly lowered his head until it touched the floor in front of him.

"Om mommanomma, om mommanomma, om mommanomma, om momm. . . ."

The transcendental meditation had seemed to stimulate his interest in things Oriental. He'd begun reading books on Hatha Yoga, and found the postures simultaneously stimulating and relaxing. Often, on a set, when he had a very minor part and there was nothing to do, he'd assumed an *arda matze-yendrasana* position, and the time had seemed to fly by. He began to read Zen, puzzling over the immutable *koans*, usually involving Chinese monks who met each other on empty roads and exchanged cryptic phrases or, better yet, meaningful silences. His interest began to wane, however, when he realized that he could not figure out the significance of any of the *koans*, a necessary step to advancement. *I could tell you the meanings*, said the author of one book, *but then your understanding would not be Zen, and you would not truly be enlightened.* Elliot had never been enlightened, although he still enjoyed keeping up certain rituals.

"Do you know," said Paula, "that it is five minutes to six?"

"Om mommanomma, om—"

"In the morning."

"Om mommanomma."

"Five to six in the morning. Isn't there a church where you can do that?"

Elliot held up a hand for her to be quiet. He was nearly finished.

"Om mommanomma, om mommanomma, om mommanomma, ommmmmm."

He touched his head a final time to the floor, then opened his eyes.

"You finished?" said Paula. "Is that the last chorus?"

"I'm in a blissful state," said Elliot. "Don't bug me, or I'll kill you."

Paula put her hands on her hips. "Is this gonna be the regular routine? Guitars at night and humming in the morning? I've been in musicals that didn't have this much music."

Carefully, Elliot folded his prayer shawl. "Miss McFadden. This morning I start rehearsals for my first New York play. It's probably the most important day of my life. My entire career may depend on it. And am I nervous, Miss McFadden?"

The insane don't get nervous, thought Paula.

"No," continued Elliot, "I am not nervous. Because I have meditated, I am calm. Because I have meditated, I am relaxed. I am confident. You, on the other hand, did *not* meditate. Therefore *you* are a pain in the ass."

He headed into the kitchen.

I'll poison his food, thought Paula, following him.

As soon as she got to the table she saw the plan would never work. Elliot had opened his duffel bag and was removing a large assortment of bottles;

65

jars, and bags. He helped himself to a small bowl from one of the kitchen cabinets.

"Today, Mr. Garfield," said Paula, "happens to be an important day for me, too."

Elliot ignored her.

"I just happen to be auditioning for a new musical this morning."

Elliot emptied the contents of three bags, four jars, and one bottle into the bowl.

"I slept seventeen minutes last night, thanks to you," said Paula, "and with the bags I have under my eyes, unless this musical is about old people, I don't have a chance in hell—Are you listening to me? What is that slop you're putting in my dishes?"

Elliot stirred the bowl with a soup spoon. "Wheat germ, soya, lecithin, natural honey, everything organic."

It figured.

"My body is a temple, and I am worshipping it."

"Well, mine's a scrap heap," said Paula, "and I'm trying to salvage it."

"This food," continued Elliot jauntily, "is what gives me my vitality, my energy, and my wonderful disposition. I happen to be sixty-three years old, Miss McFadden, and look at me."

Paula grimaced.

"Can I fix you a bowl?" said Elliot.

Paula looked at him. "This isn't going to work out, you know. I mean, I really don't know you well enough to truly dislike you, but you're just too weird to live with."

Elliot had started eating. For Paula's benefit, he consumed the food with special relish, opening his mouth extra wide, leaving the soup spoon in especially long, and grinding his jaws in exaggerated motions.

66

"Look," said Paula softly. "Why don't you try to find yourself another place, and I'll pay you back your six hundred dollars once I get a job?"

"You're forgetting," said Elliot, his mouth full. "Thish is mahpatmen and—"

"What?"

He swallowed. "This is *my* apartment. You're living here on an Elliot Garfield grant. You really ought to try this. It has whole bran in it. My feeling is that all your problems come from irregularity."

He smiled pleasantly, the interstices between his teeth plugged by pieces of sesame seeds.

Chapter 5

Paula hurried down the steps. She was upset because she was late, and she was late because she'd been upset. As she scooted by the third floor, Mr. Horvath appeared in the doorway. He was wearing a pair of blue overalls and no shirt.

"Hey! Mrs. Paula. How are you?"

"Oh, I'm fine, Mr. Horvath. Perfect. Couldn't be better."

"Thay. I want to tell you, I—"

"Mr. Horvath, could I catch you later? I'm in a big hurry now."

Horvath stepped out of the doorway. He was a big man with rimless spectacles who liked to show people the scars on his meaty arms where machine gun bullets had entered and left.

"Nevair you mind, you hurry. Latht night, I thtay up, you know why?"

Paula widened her eyes and shook her head.

"I hear radio playink, you know who ith?"

"Well—"

"You. Playink, umm, guitar. Yeth? You know?"

"It was an accident, Mr. Horvath. I have a clock radio. It went on by itself in the middle of the night. I really am sorry."

"And again he went on thith morning."

"Yes. I'm having it fixed."

"Oh, I fikth," said Horvath, laughing a meaty, lisping laugh. "You tell that radio, he go on any more by accident, young Horvath come up, break hith bones. That fikth him. Ha-ha, you get it?"

"I get it, Mr. Horvath," said Paula, walking rapidly. "Thank you."

Paula and Donna stood in the crowd of dancers. Paula estimated there were about thirty of them, all milling about outside the stage door there in Shubert Alley, waiting to be called, waiting for their chance, their break.

"Jesus! said Donna. "Every kid in New York with ten toes is here."

"They're so young," said Paula, looking around, dismayed. "Aren't they too young to work in the theater?"

"Listen," said Donna, "we have something these kids can't buy."

"I think whatever it is, I lost it," said Paula.

"Experience," said Donna. "We have experience."

"So how come I worked so much when I was a kid?" said Paula.

They were inside the theater in half an hour. Fifteen minutes after that, they were waiting backstage in the wings, having left their outer clothes on hooks in the large communal dressing room. Paula, in a leotard, began doing some limbering-up bends and kicks. Half a dozen other dancers were also loosening up nearby. Donna, in a warm-up suit, came up behind Paula and tapped her on the shoulder. "Paula?"

She gasped. "What?" Turning, she saw who it

was. "Oh, God! Jesus, you scared me! I thought it was my turn."

"How you feeling?" said Donna, doing some easy bends and stretches.

"Old," said Paula. "One foot and a few toes in the grave. I saw one girl before who goes to Lucy's school."

Donna shook her head. They walked to where they could look out at the stage. On it, three male dancers in jeans and three females in leotards were going through a complex, rigorous routine. A choreographer shouted occasional instructions, and an assistant made arcane markings on the floor. The male dancers all looked in their early twenties; two of the women couldn't have been more than teenagers. Paula looked at the tightly outlined crotches of the men. She'd seen a million of them and always wondered if it were only she who had a filthy, sex-oriented viewpoint. Could it really be that other people viewed tight crotches on dancers as simply part of the costume, and a natural, pure accompaniment of terpsichorean art? No, she thought. There must be at least a few other low-life mentalities out there. Her reverie was broken by the calling out of names. She looked up and saw that the group on stage had finished and the assistant was reading off a list.

". . . DeLurie, Jamie Fletcher, Paul Kaiser, Cynthia Robbins, Donna Douglas, and Paula McFadden. All those people on stage, please."

"Think positive," said Donna.

"Mention it to my legs," said Paula.

They walked out on stage, together with the four others called.

"All right," said the assistant. "Two rows, please. Girls in the front."

70

Paula, Donna, and a petite blonde moved forward. All of a sudden, Paula heard a voice from somewhere in the darkened theater.

"Paula?"

She squinted into the seats and finally discerned a few people near the aisle in the second and third rows.

"Paula?" came the voice again. "Is that you?"

"Yes," said Paula.

"Ronnie Burns."

"Oh. Hi, Ronnie," said Paula. A break, she thought. Then corrected herself—it would depend. She'd worked with Burns years before in a road show of *Applause* and again after that on a TV special. He was energetic, cheerful, not-too-talented, in her opinion, and once he'd asked her out on a date. She'd refused.

"I thought you gave all this up," Burns said now.

"I did," said Paula. "I just picked the wrong one to give it up for."

She could not see his expression.

"You been keeping in shape?" he asked.

What the hell was this, thought Paula. A public confession? "Oh, listen," she said. "Terrific."

Burns leaned back in his seat. "You wanna show me?"

"Can I take the written test instead?"

She thought she heard a chuckle, and then Burns said, "Okay, Eddie."

Eddie raised his hands. "Just a few basic impossible steps, kids, so pay attention."

He showed them a short routine and led them into it. Everyone, including Paula and Donna, seemed to pick it up right. The problem was that as the music quickened, Paula began to lag behind the others. Her legs would simply put commands

71

from her brain on "hold" while they recovered from the earlier efforts. The pace became still more vigorous, and Paula's lag became more noticeable. When the music stopped, she was breathing very heavily—gasping, really—and just about exhausted.

"I went from age thirty-three to ninety-seven in two minutes thirty seconds," she managed to say after some time had passed.

She looked over at the others. Except for Donna, who reclined on the floor, the rest might have just been out for a leisurely stroll. *Damn kids. Why aren't they in school?* Two of them were doing calisthenics. The other two were laughing and talking. We need a union, thought Paula. The Amalgamated Aged Dancers of America. No admission under thirty. Protect us from our cursed youth.

Eddie had crossed to the stage apron and was talking to Burns. He looked up now and checked his clipboard. "Robert DeLurie and Cynthia Robbins, please wait. The rest of you, thank you for coming in."

Paula had turned to leave, when she heard Burns' voice. "A little rusty, Paula, but not bad. My problem is I need 'em very young."

"Young?" said Paula, with mock ingenuousness. "Oh, okay . . . I'll work on it."

She thought: I still wouldn't go out with you, creep. She walked off.

Elliot sat with the rest of the actors in a semicircle facing a table behind which sat Mark Bodine, the director.

They were in the basement of a church on 2nd Street, and despite the fact that two hundred fifty seats had been installed, and the place was billed as a "theater," it was still the basement of the

72

Church-of-All-Countries on 2nd Street. Three years before, one of the actors had told Elliot, the basement had held an indoor swimming pool. For fifty cents you could rent a locker and a 1906-vintage bathing suit with one shoulder strap and swim to your heart's content in ice-cold water so chlorinated it would turn brown eyes blue. Now, in that same location, you could watch *Richard III*. Which, though Elliot, the way this is going, might be worse than being bleached.

The actors held their scripts in their hands, occasionally taking a desultory glance at the table where Mark Bodine sat, gesturing animatedly as he discussed the play.

Bodine was a mid-thirtyish, gawky man with a disheveled, unkempt appearance. Part of the reason for this was because he was disheveled and unkempt, but the effect was heightened by a peculiar hairstyle, a kind of radial Afro, in which zillions of limp, lengthy corkscrews seemed to be hurrying away from his scalp. His speech—a scholarly, pedantic whine—was punctuated by particularly ineffectual, wispy, brushing motions by which he attempted to block one or another of the corkscrews from interfering with his vision.

"Now then, what about Richard? The question is, and this may seem perfunctory, was Richard actually deformed? Historically we know that he was born with a severe curvature of the spine, giving the impression that he was hunchbacked. There was some paralysis of the left hand and right foot. Olivier chose right hand and left foot, God only knows why. And nerve damage—"

This is unbelievable, thought Elliot. The man thinks he's Marcus Welby. Here we are, sitting, trying to do a simple play about Richard III—all

73

right, not simple exactly, but straightforward enough —and this guy is converting it to a medical nightmare. Pretty soon we'll hear how Richard had tic douloureux and Blount's Syndrome and a hernia when he was six, and we can forget about the play entirely. We can do a psychodrama for the AMA.

"—to the right cheek and eyelids. I mean, the man was your basic gimp, let's face it."

This guy, thought Elliot, would probably refer to Einstein as "your basic klutz."

Bodine droned on. "Which brings us, bless the wise and rich Mrs. Estelle Morganweiss, to this production. Is that how we want to play Richard?"

"That's how I want to play it," whispered Elliot to a small, snub-faced actor named O'Boyle, sitting next to him.

"If you do," said Bodine, swiping dreamily at an errant curlicue, "this director would prefer to do a six-week stint on the Sonny and Cher show. Richard the Third was a flaming homosexual."

Elliot groaned, then quickly coughed to cover it.

"So was Shakespeare, for that matter," said Bodine, "but that angry crowd at the Globe theater was not going to put down two shillings just to see a bunch of pansies jumping around on the stage. No, kids, it was society that crippled Richard, and not birth. I mean, read your text. He sent those two cute young boys up to the Tower, and no one ever saw them again. We know why, don't we?"

Elliot felt sick. Why did people have to *change* things? Act the damn play the way it was written. Shakespeare knew what he was doing. He didn't need Bodine to help him out.

"What I want to do," said the director, looking up now, a lofty, magisterial expression on his face, "is strip Richard bare."

Oh, God, no! thought Elliot.

"Metaphorically," continued Bodine, with a condescending smile. "Let's get rid of the hump. Let's get rid of the twisted extremities and show him as he would be today. The queen who wanted to be king!"

The actors and actresses looked at each other, mumbling. Elliot's hand shot up.

"Yes," said Bodine.

"Question. Are you serious?"

"What's your objection, Elliot?"

"Well, number one, I have to play it. Number two, I like the hump and the club foot. And number three, I've been working on it for three months."

"Oh!" said the director, flailing at an eyebrow. "Well, I respect that. That's why we're here, to exchange ideas."

He's feigning reasonableness, thought Elliot.

"Tell me," said Bodine pleasantly, "how do you see Richard? Mr. Macho, is that it?"

"I don't think," said Elliot, "that he should be middle linebacker for the Chicago Bears or"—a name popped into his mind—"another Alan-the-horse-Ameche, but let's not toss away one of his prime motivations."

"What's that?"

"He wants to hump Lady Anne."

A few people in the class tittered, and Bodine smirked. "I've heard *that* before. Look, I don't want to press, but let's just try it my way. Why don't we read through the first act? Please! Trust me."

Elliot breathed deeply and looked around. His eyes met and held the gaze of the actress who was playing Lady Anne. He looked up.

75

"All right," he sighed. "How far off the diving board do you want me to go?"

"Well," said Bodine, thrusting out his chest, "don't give me Bette Midler, but let's not be afraid to be bold."

Elliot nodded. "Bold."

The company opened their scripts. The stage manager, a swarthy man named Ralph, said in very official tones, "Act one, scene one, enter Richard, Duke of Gloucester."

Everyone's eyes turned toward Elliot. Elliot felt his mind suddenly go completely empty, his body become devoid of feeling. *Paralyzed!* he thought. *I've gone paralyzed.* He could play Richard the Third as a paraplegic. He coughed, then found that he could squirm in his seat. *Richard the Squirmer.* He had no ideas. He'd forgotten everything he was planning to do. The others watched him intently.

"Now is—" said Elliot. *"Now* is . . . now is— can we take a five-minute break?"

He sat with Rhonda at the counter in the luncheonette.

"I'll have a toasted English," she told the counter man. "And coffee."

"Same," said Elliot.

A large cockroach ran up one wall and disappeared in a fissure in the ceiling. "If those things were our size," said Elliot, "they'd rule the world."

"Some people think they already do," said Rhonda.

She looked at him and smiled. She was a classic beauty—oval face, auburn hair, dimples, perfect body, slim legs. In two years she'd be modeling for girdle advertisements in the Sears catalogue.

"Tell you something," she said, when they had

their coffee. "You were the only one in there who had any guts. I mean, we all thought he was nutsy, but you were the only person to say something."

"Listen," said Elliot, "it's not guts, it's fear. Fear of making an ass of myself in front of hundreds of people. Notice I don't say thousands, because I don't think we're going to play to thousands. In fact, maybe I should revise that downward to dozens."

"It's ridiculous," said Rhonda, tossing her hair in a certain wonderful way that made Elliot feel weak-kneed. "It wouldn't matter if you were playing it alone in the shower."

Elliot stared at her. She'd approached *him* at the end of the session and asked if he felt like coffee. Now, as they finished, he asked her bluntly, "Listen, how about coming over to my place and doing some rehearsing? Maybe we can salvage something yet."

"Fine," she said brightly.

It was the first good thing that had happened to him since he hit New York.

In the bedroom, Paula lay prone in pajamas, with Lucy sitting on her ankles, eating an apple and studying French from a torn yellow review book. Paula grunted and, hands behind head, struggled to a sitting position.

"Thirty-seven," she said, puffing, and plopping back down. The floor felt terrific. Very supportive, the floor, thought Paula. Floors were wonderful— flat, silent, and they held you up. The trouble with sit-ups was the same as it had always been. Her right-side stomach muscles were stronger than her left-side ones, and so, as the exercise progressed, the sit-ups tended to become lean-ups. She took another breath. "Thirty-eight." Down. "Thirty-nine." Mmm. Uh. Down. "For-for-forty."

She collapsed. "That's all. I can't do any more."

"Sixty," said Lucy, biting hard into her apple. "You said sixty."

"The muscles," said Paula. "The muscles are gone. I can't dance. It was a dumb idea. I'm gonna put you up for adoption. Get me a Coke."

"Uh-uh," said Lucy. "Fattening."

"Get me the Coke, sweetheart. Mother doesn't want to beat the crap out of you."

Paula rose as Lucy left the room. "Bring it to me," she yelled. "I'll be in the bath." She went into the bathroom.

Lucy walked to the kitchen, missing by seconds the opening of the front door.

Elliot entered first, then turned to Rhonda, and curtsied elaborately.

"Enter, sweet Anne."

Rhonda walked in and looked around. "You live alone?"

"Yes," said Elliot, shutting the door. "Fortunately, the other people who live here also live alone. Let me have your coat."

She handed him her coat, which he flung over a couch. He glanced again at her figure—good breasts made even better by perfect posture; curved, flaring hips; nice, protruding ass. A ripe fruit, he thought, waiting to be picked by a Chicago actor.

"Come." He reached for her hand and led her toward the kitchen.

Lucy, who had just opened the refrigerator, turned, startled, as Elliot and Rhonda walked in.

"Hi, Lucy," said Elliot. "This is Rhonda. Rhonda, Lucy. Lucy, Rhonda, Rhonda, Lucy."

He bent over and extracted two Cokes from the refrigerator.

"Hi," said Lucy.

"Hello," said Rhonda.

Elliot grabbed two glasses from a cabinet. "Whatcha doin'?" he asked Lucy.

"Sitting on my mother," said Lucy, staring unabashedly at Rhonda.

"Sounds like fun," said Elliot. "Try to keep it quiet, though. Rhonda and I will be working in my bedroom."

He pushed gently past Lucy with the Coke-filled glasses and steered Rhonda toward the hall.

"Good night," said Rhonda.

"Good night," said Lucy.

She watched them disappear behind the door of Elliot's bedroom. "I'll bet," she said aloud.

In the bathroom, Paula soaked in the tub, a towel wrapped around her head to protect her hair. Oh great basin of heated water, she thought, restore the strength, youth, and vitality to this wretched husk of a body. Okay, forget the youth and vitality. Just gimme a tiny bit strength. The door flew open and Lucy entered, carrying a Coke.

"Did I hear voices?" said Paula. "I thought I heard voices. Was that him?"

"Uh-huh," said Lucy. "He took two Cokes."

She handed Paula her drink, then picked up her French review book and sat on the hamper.

"I think these things come ripped," said Lucy. "I think they sell them all torn."

"Did you write it down?" asked Paula.

"No," said Lucy. "I didn't even notice it. Besides, once you pay for it, they wouldn't take it back even if the pages were blank."

"No, I mean the Cokes."

"Oh. No, I didn't. I didn't have a pencil."

"I told you," said Paula. "Write everything down. If he takes a glass of water, write it down. A napkin, an egg, a piece of toilet paper—"

"Huh?"

"Well, you can estimate. I just don't want him getting the idea this is a hotel."

"I don't think he'll have that idea." Lucy glanced down at the review book. "Why don't you like him?"

"Who invited him?" said Paula quickly. She leaned back and sipped her Coke. "That's why I don't like him."

"*Je vois*," said Lucy.

"What?"

"I see. *Je vois, tu vois, il voit, elle voit. Vous voyez. Nous voyons. Ils*—if he were a lawyer or a doctor instead of an actor, would you like him?"

"I wouldn't like him if I liked him," said Paula. "He annoys me."

"I think he's kinda cute," said Lucy. "He reminds me of a dog that nobody wants." She waited for the outburst, which Paula obligingly supplied.

"You are *never* to think he's cute, you hear? Never! Never! What'd he take two Cokes for, the hog?"

Lucy looked into her book and spoke nonchalantly. "One for him, one for her."

Paula's eyes widened. Her towel turban began to come unraveled. "What her?"

"He's got a girl in there," said Lucy in the same nonchalant tone. "I saw him take her in."

Paula rose in all her splendid, Charley-horsed nakedness. Her mouth tightened. "In my house? *He's got a girl in the bedroom?*"

What's so bad? thought Lucy. It's not as if he was keeping a gorilla, or army ants.

"Why didn't you say something?" said Paula.

"I'm sorry," said Lucy, unflustered. "You want me to write girls down, too?"

Paula grabbed her robe and stormed out. She pounded at the door of Elliot's bedroom, which opened almost immediately. Elliot stood there grinning, Coke in hand. Behind him, seated on the bed, Rhonda was holding her play script.

"I thought I heard a knock," said Elliot. "Was it my imagination?"

"Can I speak to you in private?" said Paula, unsmiling.

"Gee, it's a bad time," said Elliot. "How about at breakfast?"

Paula looked over his shoulder, straining to see in the dim light. "Is that a girl in there?"

Elliot looked back, as if to check. "Uh, let's see. Yes. Yes, I believe so."

"Not," said Paula with soft intensity, "in my house. I won't put up with this sort of thing."

Elliot grinned. "I don't understand. You have a girl in your room and I don't object."

Snippity bastard. Paula felt like punching him.

"Rhonda," said Elliot blithely, still with that cocky, tongue-in-cheek expression, "this is Miss McFadden. Mac lives just down the bedroom a piece. Miss McFadden, this is Rhonda Fontana, a gifted and rising young actress. Don't rise!"

"Hi," said Rhonda, from the bed. She seemed completely untroubled.

"Hello," said Paula curtly. Then, to Elliot, "Can we talk? This is serious."

Elliot knitted his brows and assumed an expression of mock gravity. He smiled, however, to

Rhonda before he stepped out into the hall and closed the door behind him.

Paula stood with her hands on her hips and her lips pressed together hard. "Out!"

"Out? No, I thought he was safe."

"Her—out! They have motels for that sort of activity! I have an impressionable ten-year-old daughter in there, and this is not one of the impressions I want her picking up. Now, you get that rising young actress up and float her the hell out of there!"

And then what? thought Elliot. Do my homework, take out the garbage, and go to sleep with my milk and a cookie? This poor woman still doesn't comprehend her situation.

"Out of where?" he said now, for the first time really angry. "Out of *my* rented apartment that you're staying in out of the kindness of *my* heart?"

Paula tried to maintain a level stare, but felt herself beginning to falter. Why am I so weak? she thought. Why can't I even bluff? I should take lessons from Nixon. I should stonewall it, tough it out.

"I will," continued Elliot deliberately, "bring home anyone or anything I choose, including a one-eyed Episcopalian kangaroo, if that be my kinky inclination. As to what's going on in there, not that it's any of your business, we happen to be rehearsing act one, scene four from *Richard the Third*. I have a cretin from Mars directing this play, and I need all the extra work I can get."

Paula could no longer look at him. He was too strong; she was beaten.

Elliot pressed his advantage relentlessly, homing in on the central issue. "However, if I choose to attempt to have carnal knowledge of that gorgeous

82

bod, that will be my problem, her option, and none of your beeswax!"

He pivoted and started for the door, then turned back. "And just for the record, what was little Lucy's impression of what was going on for twelve months in Momma's bedroom with Tony "Love-'em-and-leave-'em' DeForrest? She thought you were making gingerbread cookies, maybe?"

He looked at her sternly. "Turn out the lights, will ya? We're running up a hell of a bill."

Elliot turned and walked back into his room, closing the door behind him. In the darkened hallway, the tears slid down Paula's cheeks and dripped onto the collar of her robe.

"The woman is unbelievable," said Elliot. "She's staying here purely through my good graces, benevolence, humanity, and sweet temper, and yet she persists in busting my . . . chops."

"She seemed a little uptight," said Rhonda softly. "Oh, well, you want to continue?" She looked down at the script. "Let's see, I think we left off——"

"Ah," said Elliot, "let's take a break. That whole thing got me out of the mood." He inhaled and caught Rhonda's perfume, a musk scent that was not too subtle.

Rhonda put down her script. "Is she your . . . you know?"

"What?" said Elliot.

"Well, mistress, I guess."

"Her?" Elliot laughed. "Her? Are you serious?"

"Why? She's not bad-looking."

"Oh, no," said Elliot. "No, we don't—we were just flung together through some kind of fluke accident. We get along like oil and water."

Rhonda was leaning back on one elbow. Her

breasts stood out prominently against the thin material of her blouse. She appeared very comfortable and relaxed.

"Uh, would you mind if I took off my shirt?" said Elliot. "It's very warm in here, and I'm used to walking around in the buff."

"Doesn't bother me," said Rhonda.

Pliant, thought Elliot. That's the word for her. He stripped off his shirt and flung it on a dresser. "You know what's killing me?" he said.

Rhonda slowly shook her head. She followed him with her eyes.

"My back. Really killing me, right here." He put one arm behind him and grabbed at himself about a third of the way down. "I was out in the rain last night, and I must've caught a chill, or something. Really murderous. You ever have anything like that?"

Rhonda nodded slowly. She looked amused. "And you want me to rub it, correct?"

"That would be a truly humanitarian gesture toward a fellow actor," said Elliot. "I'd be happy to reciprocate, of course."

Rhonda moved over to him. "What do I get for this, besides your reciprocity, of course?"

"Well . . ." said Elliot, as the touch of her soft hands on his shoulder blades sent a soaring erotic charge through him. "God!"

"What?"

"Uh . . . let's see. How about a serenade? You massage—uh, oooh, ohh—I serenade."

"Fair enough," she said. "But you still have to reciprocate."

"Oh, sure," said Elliot, grabbing up his guitar, which was within arm's reach. Her hands are like a sculptor's, he thought. This is almost as good as

screwing right here. "Listen, fair's fair. Tit for tat."
He looked around slyly.

In the kitchen, Paula made a specially loud racket
as she scooped some herring tidbits into a bowl for
Lucy. She opened the refrigerator door and removed
a container of milk, then slammed the door closed.
She put a few Oreos on a plate, then placed everything—milk glasses, cookies, bowl—on a platter
and turned off the light. Carefully, she carried the
platter to her bedroom.

"You okay?" said Lucy.

Paula placed the herring on Lucy's night table.
"I'm fine. You can have this, then go to sleep."

"You upset because they're messing around in
there?"

"They are not messing around," said Paula. "They
are doing act one, scene four from *Richard the
Third*." She hesitated. "Lucy, did it ever bother
you about Tony and me? I mean, not being married
and living together."

"No. . . ." said Lucy.

"I wanted to get married, you know," said Paula.
"But he couldn't get a divorce."

Lucy stabbed up a chunk of herring with her
fork. "That's okay."

"I just wanted to know how you felt." She patted
her daughter on the head. "You know?"

Lucy nodded. "Are you gonna eat your Oreos?"

"You can have them." Paula handed Lucy the
plate. "Just watch the crumbs. And turn off the light
when you're through." She leaned over and kissed
Lucy on the forehead. "Good night, angel."

"Night," said Lucy.

A minute later, the soft sounds of a guitar came

wafting in from the other bedroom—a Spanish melody of love.

"Is that song from *Richard the Third*?" whispered Lucy.

Chapter 6

They lay on their backs, their legs extended stiffly out in front of them, four inches off the floor. Marian had been merciless today, and even the kids were sweating profusely and grunting with the effort of the workout.

"Hold that position!" said Marian sternly, walking between the rows of people. "You hold that now!"

Paula was in agony; two full minutes in this posture was simply beyond their capability. She gritted her teeth, closed her eyes, and finally gave up.

Marian, passing, silently shook her head.

Well, if you'd been up all night to the sound of bouncing bedsprings in the next room, you couldn't hold the position, either, thought Paula. The night had been even a more exquisite form of torture than the leg raises. A man and a woman, strangers, a few steps away, making violent, passionate love, while Paula lay there and tossed and turned. Tony had been away only two days, and already she ached with loneliness. It was impossible not to imagine what they were doing, to see it in her mind's eye, to feel it, even, his hands moving over her body, squeezing her, his fingers exploring, prodding, caressing. A night of torture and yearning. Bastard. The lousy, self-centered, insensitive boor.

"Oh, please God," she said aloud, when Marian at last signaled the end of the exercise, "let me be hit by a rich man in a Rolls-Royce."

"I think I can arrange it," said Donna, who'd collapsed next to her.

"Thank you," said Paula. A droplet of perspiration rolled onto her upper lip, and she licked it off.

"No, I'm serious," said Donna, "I mean, it's funny you should say that."

"What'd I say?"

"There's an outside chance," said Donna, "that I can get us both a job at the Auto Show at the Coliseum. It's not only two weeks' work, but the money's not bad."

"*Any* money's not bad," said Paula. Then, suddenly, a suspicious look came over her face. "Wait a minute . . . wait a minute! What do we have to do?"

Donna grinned. "Oh, it's very simple. We'll be introduced to one or two guys—all older men—and all we have to—" She broke off, laughing as she saw Paula's expression. "No, no, I'm just kidding. Really. No, all we have to do is look pretty and point to the cars."

"Whew," said Paula. "That, I can do. I'm a terrific pointer."

"And they give you some little thing you have to say," said Donna. "Very short. But no dancing, no bending."

"I can do that, too," said Paula. "I'm terrific at not dancing and bending." She leaned close to Donna. "As long as there's no fu—"

"None," said Donna. She looked up. "Unless you wanna get paid, of course." She laughed, and so did Paula. "This friend of mine will let me know this weekend. Just keep it quiet."

Paula, very suddenly, felt an overwhelming urge to cry. "What a nice person you are," she told Donna, swallowing hard. "You didn't have to tell me."

Donna looked at her sympathetically. "Well, you know. We were both given the shaft, literal and figurative, by your ex-husband. I feel related."

Paula smiled.

"All right, you lazy good-for-nothings," said Marian. "Everybody up, break's over!"

"What break?" said Paula. "There was a break?"

In an area that had once been identified by the four-foot-deep marker of a swimming pool, Rhonda Fontana, feeling remarkably relaxed and fulfilled, was addressing two shlumpy-looking coffin bearers in her role as Lady Anne.

"If ever he have wife, let her be made
More miserable by the death of him
Than I am made by my young lord and thee!
Come, now toward Chertsey with your holy load.
Taken from Paul's to be interred there.
And still, as you are weary of this weight,
Rest you, whiles I lament King Henry's corse."

From offstage right, Elliot came striding on, or perhaps *mincing* on would be a better description. Or *prancing*. He was without hump or any other noticeable deformity.

"Stay, you that bear the corse," said Elliot prissily, in a nasal voice, "and set it down."

Rhonda's eyes lit up with suppressed laughter as she spoke.

"What black magician conjures up this fiend
To stop devoted charitable deeds?"

Oh, Christ, thought Elliot. Oh here I go!

"Villains," he said. "Set down the corse, or by
Saint Paul, I'll make a corse of him that disobeys!"

A menacing homosexual, thought Elliot. The
most challenging role of my life. I might as well
play a menacing eggnog or an aggressive Japanese
pine.

"My lord," said the First Gentleman. "Stand
back and let the coffin pass."

Elliot assumed an expression not quite stern, so
that the overall, undesired effect was mournful.

"Unmannered dog! Stand'st thou when I com-
     mand?
Advance thy halberd higher than my breast,
Or, by Saint Paul, I'll strike thee to my foot."

And suddenly, in one breath, he gave up.

"My careereth is over," he said, barely pausing.
"I am making a horseth asseth of myselfeth."

"Huh?" said Rhonda.

Elliot turned to Bodine, who was hovering nearby.
"Mark, I beg you. If you want this kind of performance, let me play Lady Anne."

"All right, everybody!" yelled Bodine loudly.
"Let's take a break! Back in ten minutes. Ten."

He walked away, motioning with his head for
Elliot to follow him. "Let's get some air," he said.

They passed through a long, dank hallway, and
Elliot imagined he could still smell that in-

door pool odor, chlorine-mixed-with-stale-water-old towels-and-athletes'-foot. They found a flight of narrow metal steps and walked up.

"What a shithole," said Mark.

"Hey," said Elliot. "This is a church."

"Doesn't change things," said Mark. "Maybe it's a holy shithole, but that doesn't alter its basic character."

They emerged into a small vestibule and immediately stepped outside. The sun shone with a blazing yellow brightness in a cloudless cerulean sky.

"Speaking of character," said Mark, "you're unhappy, Elliot, aren't you?"

"Unhappy?" said Elliot. "No, not unhappy. Freakin' petrified."

The director put an arm around him.

Elliot thought: I'm going to interpret this as a simple gesture of man-to-man openness and friendship. That's all there is to it. This man is in touch with his emotions, and he's forthright and outgoing in his expression of them. It's me that's the sickie for even beginning to imagine that there could. . . .

"The critics will crucify me Mark," he said, "and the Gay Liberation are gonna hang me from Shakespeare's statue by my genitalia. You gotta help me, Mark."

Mark spoke softly. "What do you want, Elliot?"

"I want my hump back," Elliot whined. "I want my club foot, I want a little paralysis in my right hand. It doesn't have to be a lot. Two stiff fingers . . . I need motivation."

"I see," said Mark coldly. He withdrew the arm. "In other words, you want to play it safe. You want to give us your standard, conventional Richard. I can't argue with that, Elliot. It's perfectly reasonable. They've been doing it that way for four hundred years."

Elliot felt like one of the standees along the banks of the Hudson, laughing like a hyena as poor Fulton struggled on the water with his steamboat. "Listen," he said now, "what do I know? I'm lucky I got the part."

"No, no," said Bodine, "not luck."

"I'm from Chicago," said Elliot. "We act differently out there. We try to do the plays as written. If that doesn't go down in New York, terrific. I respect you. You've done off-Broadway, I haven't. I'm not a quitter. I'll play Richard like Tatum O'Neal, if you want. But . . . don't let me look foolish out there."

"Is it so bad to look foolish?" said Mark. "Is that the worst thing in the world?"

"Well . . . maybe not the worst. I mean, maybe it's topped by angina, or delivering a baby, or sinus drainings, but it's right up there."

"And you *feel* foolish?"

Elliot became aware of a kind of patronizing, psychiatric tone in Mark's voice. It annoyed him. "I feel like an asshole," he said. "I passed foolish on Tuesday."

Mark aimed an index finger at a strand of hair directly over his left eyelid. He thrust and missed. "We have to trust each other, Elliot."

Trust goes against the grain of all my previous experience, thought Elliot. "I do," he lied.

"I was never going to let you do it like that," said Mark.

Elliot sighed and let his head loll to one side. "Thank God!"

"But you do see where I'm heading?" said Bodine.

"I'm trying, Mark," said Elliot, determined now

92

to concentrate. Had he missed some basic point all along?

"Richard was gay," said Bodine flatly. "There's no doubt about that. But let's use that as the subtext. We'll keep it, but now we can put back the hump and the club foot."

"And the twisted fingers?" said Elliot, hoping against hope. It was a kind of *Medical Center* in reverse.

"If you like them," said Mark graciously.

"I love them!" said Elliot. "Crazy about 'em."

"Then use them, baby," said Mark intently. "Use them. And then you'll see what I'm after. Try it my way, bubula. I'll never let you go wrong."

He turned to Elliot and hugged him briefly, in what, for him, was a gesture of reassurance.

They went back inside to Rhonda, who looked at the floor and returned to her original mark.

"Rhonda," said Bodine, "take it from your last line before Richard's entrance."

Rhonda paused, and cleared her throat. "Rest you, whiles I lament King Henry's corse."

Elliot reentered as Richard, hunched over, dragging his club foot, his right hand hanging limply at his side. He also swished slightly as he moved, and pursed his lips. I am, he thought, the weirdest, most afflicted Richard who ever lived. Or died.

"Stay, you that bear the corse, and set it down."

Rhonda, though trained in self-control and though particularly sensitive to Elliot's predicament, could stand it no longer. She burst out in wild shrieks of hysterical, high-pitched laughter.

In aisle six, Paula stopped and put a can of creamed corn in her cart. She remembered how, years before, she used to ride Lucy on the little shelf, her chubby legs pushing down into the basket. The little girl would reach for things as they passed and occasionally identify products in her baby-pidgin English. Never again, thought Paula, wistfully. No more children for Paula McFadden.

In aisle seven, Elliot moved rapidly and purposefully. His low point of the day had passed. Now he could look forward to tomorrow's low point. As he rounded frozen meats, he found himself locked cart against cart with Paula

"Hey! I know you from somewhere."

"Please," said Paula. "I enjoy shopping. It's one of the last things I have left. Don't spoil *this* for me, too."

Actually, it was a lie, said for effect. The only people who really enjoyed shopping were those who didn't have to do it all the time. Like actors in those lyrical movie scenes where the young-couple-in-love traipse joyously down the supermarket aisles, gleefully snatching up the margarines and bathroom cleaners and frozen pizzas.

"Relax," said Elliot. "We don't have to fight until we get home." He pulled a list from his pocket and stared. "We need soap, darling."

"Not in *my* bathroom," said Paula. She reached for a can of stringbeans, examined it, then put it back.

"Look," said Elliot, "this is silly. If you buy what you need and I buy what I need, we could blow a lot of bread buying the same things . . . including bread. Why don't we have one shopping list and then split up the bill?"

The logic, Elliot thought smugly, is impeccable.

"On what items?" Paula said suspiciously.

"Food, kitchen and bathroom cleansers, and all household products."

Paula narrowed her eyes.

"Any male and female doodads are excepted," added Elliot quickly. *I don't pay for your little tampons, you don't chip in for my rubber goods.* "There, you go your way, and I'll go mine."

"And we split everything?" said Paula.

"Everything," said Elliot, and then, keeping a straight face: "I'll pay my full one-third share."

Paula did a slow take. "*One third*!!"

"I'm not the one with a daughter," said Elliot sweetly.

"What's the matter?" said Paula. "Didn't Lady Anne wash her hands the other night?"

Elliot smiled in appreciation. "Quick! Quick! I love a quick girl." He opened wide his arms. "Okay. Down the middle."

He began to take items out of her cart and put them into his. At the check-out counter, Paula picked up a *TV Guide* and a package of gum.

"What's that for?" said Elliot.

"What?"

"The *TV Guide*?"

"You don't know what this is for?" Paula said. "It guides you to the TV."

"We really don't need it."

"But I *want* it."

"Separate payment?"

"You can use it, too."

"But I rarely watch TV," said Elliot, "and besides, I don't need a guide. I know where the set is."

"Forget it," said Paula. "I'll pay."

"What about the gum?"

"What about it?"

"Is that joint gum?"

"Yes. All right. Yes."

"I don't chew gum."

"Well, learn."

"Okay, give me a piece."

Paula tossed him the package, and Elliot extracted a stick.

"Cash or charge?" said the cashier.

"Treasury notes," said Elliot. "Ninety-day maturity."

"Cash," said Paula.

When they were packed and each had two bags, Elliot placed the stick of gum in Paula's mouth. "Very bad for you," he said. "Rots your teeth."

"If you were really concerned about my health," said Paula, "you'd book an immediate flight to Angola."

Outside, they headed toward home at a brisk pace. As they passed a liquor store, Elliot said, "Hold it! Chianti! Can't have spaghetti marinara without a little *vino*."

Paula continued walking. "You can on my budget."

Elliot put a hand on her shoulder, stopping her. "Please. I'll blow for the booze. Short of stature, but not tight of pocket. I'll be right out."

Paula waited outside while Elliot entered the store.

"Can I help you?" said the salesman, a red-faced, balding individual.

"A bottle of your finest cheap Chianti, please."

"How cheap you wanna go?"

"Mmm, one-eighty top."

"Jesus, that's cheap. For one-eighty, you can't even get grapejuice."

"You can," said Elliot. "I just bought some."

"Well, you'd be better off with that," said the salesman. "Let's see, for one-eighty I could give you . . . mmm . . . a California Red."

"Nothing from Kansas?" said Elliot.

The salesman held up his hand. "Listen, do me a favor. You willing to go up to two-fifty?"

"With or without tax?"

"What do I look like? Al Capone? Without. The tax is additional."

"Well. . . ."

"Trust me on this," said the salesman. "You won't be sorry. I know this grower personally. I drink the stuff myself. Listen, to me, what's the difference between one-eighty and two-fifty?"

"Probably what it is to me," said Elliot. "About seventy cents."

"Exactly the point!" said the salesman, pulling a bottle off the shelf. "Friend, you have an exciting adventure awaiting you."

Elliot paid for the wine and headed out.

Emerging from the store, he caught sight of Paula flat up against the building, grocery bags fallen to the ground, their contents strewn over the sidewalk. She appeared to be in shock—ashen, lips working, gasping for air.

Elliot rushed over and grabbed her shoulders. "What is it? What's wrong?"

"My bag!" Paula finally was able to whimper. "They took my bag!"

"Groceries?"

"No. My pocketbook."

"Who did?"

Paula pointed weakly to a distant blue automobile. "In the car. There were two of them."

"Jesus!" said Elliot.

"One jumped out and grabbed my bag." She twisted her head and neck and closed her eyes in anguish. "I had everything in it."

"Jesus!" said Elliot again. "Dirty bastards."

97

Paula snapped suddenly awake. "Aren't you going to go after them?"

"After a speeding car?"

Her mood seemed instantly to change. "Thanks!" She was furious. "Thanks a lot!" She bent down and began to pick up her spilled groceries.

"They could be armed," said Elliot. "What do you want me to do, fight it out with a can of tomato paste?" He held up the can.

She grabbed it away from him and got on her hands and knees. "Leave me alone. *Just leave me alone.*"

Elliot shrugged. The woman, quite clearly, was a loon.

Ten minutes later, he was walking two steps behind her as Paula, pausing only to wipe tears and blow her nose, headed angrily up 78th Street.

"I still think you ought to go to the police and report it," he called ahead. "I could call, if you want."

"I wish," said Paula, "you were that helpful while I was being robbed."

"Listen," said Elliot. "I'm sorry, but I didn't see a thing. Kill me, I was in the store. What do you want from me, anyway? I'm not a German Shepherd."

Paula walked faster, and Elliot stopped. He stared at her, fuming, just as a blue car sped past.

Paula shrieked. "Oh! Oh, my God! It's them! IT'S THEM!"

"Who?"

"The ones who took my bag!" She ran after the car. "STOP THEM! Somebody, stop them!"

She continued to run, yelling and screaming at the top of her lungs, struggling to hold on to her groceries. For a moment, Elliot stood stunned, rooted in place. Then, setting down his bags, he took off after the car, sprinting at top speed. In seconds, he'd passed Paula and had almost caught up to a dented blue Buick, which moved leisurely down the street.

Elliot had a churning, high-kneed style of running that was showy, but not really fast. He felt the breath pound in and out of his chest, felt the back of his throat become hot and dry. He came to a curb, pushed off, and vaulted onto the opposite sidewalk. He was dimly aware of passersby stopping to watch him, frozen as he flashed past, a timeless fresco. He was managing, somehow, to keep pace with the Buick, but not really gaining on it. He ran on, feeling the weight come suddenly into his legs, conscious of the blood throbbing through his temples. *Actor Victim of Heart Attack*, read the headline in his brain. My body is a temple, he thought, and I'm pissing on it.

Ahead, the Buick had slowed. A red Impala was stopped in front of it, waiting at a light. A man stepped into Elliot's path.

"Out of my way!" said Elliot, grabbing the man by the shoulders and thrusting him aside. "I'm gonna get a bullet right between my goddamn eyes!"

He reached the Buick and jerked open the front door on the driver's side. Two men sat in the front seat, both white. A black man reclined in the back.

"All right," said Elliot, breathing heavily, amazed at his own bravado. "Give it to me. *Gimme her bag!* Come on, goddammit, I'm not afraid of you guys, get out of the car! Move!" To his own ears, he sounded good, a Broderick Crawford type of hard-boiled detective.

The driver, however, was apparently unfamiliar with Crawford. He looked amused. "Okay," he said, "we surrender."

The other man in front, unsmiling, said, "Piss off, piss-head!"

The driver turned to the man in back. "Grab him, Cookie. Let's take him."

The man in back opened his door.

Elliot backed rapidly away. "All right, don't get excited! I was just asking! I was just asking!"

At that moment, the light turned green and the red Impala ahead drove off. The man in back closed his door.

"Have a pleasant day," said the Buick driver as he slowly pulled away.

Elliot stood alone in the street. Groups of children were watching him from the sidewalk, laughing, pointing, and gesturing.

"Freaking humiliating," he said to no one in particular, as he began to walk back to Paula.

The route back seemed a lot longer now than when he'd first run it. Occasionally, people stared at him. He suppressed the impulse to hang his head. When he got to Paula, he found her again on her hands and knees. Close by was one of her paper bags, split neatly in half. He bent to join her.

"I had all my money in there," she said, crying bitterly, scarcely noticing him. "Everything! My last dollar in the world!"

Elliot felt genuinely moved.

"You and your goddamn Chianti," said Paula, sniffing and swiping at a tear.

The sympathy drained from him. "What's Chianti got to do with it? You could at least thank me for risking my life for you." He began to help her retrieve the fallen groceries.

"Did you get my bag back?" Paula went on. "No! So why should I thank you? Why do I have such lousy luck every time an actor comes into my life? I hate all of you!"

Elliot leaned over to pick up a can she was reaching for, but she pushed him aside.

"Get away from me! Get away!"

She took the last few items in her arms, stood up, and began walking down the block. Elliot followed meekly.

"I really don't think they robbed you because I'm an actor," he said.

Chapter 7

The three of them sat around the table. Lucy twirled seventy-four linear feet of spaghetti on her fork. Elliot drank his two-fifty-plus-tax Chianti, and Paula sulked. Her food, barely touched, lay cold and congealing in front of her. Elliot had made the spaghetti himself, entranced as he always was with the flame on the burner, the *process* of the food actually cooking. Hypnotized, he'd watched the food steadily, barely pulling out of his reverie to turn off the gas when the spaghetti was done. Two candles burned on the table as he spoke animatedly to Lucy.

". . . then after I got out of Northwestern, I got my first summer job in Lake Michigan. Ten plays in ten weeks. Worked like a dog. I had hepatitis and the mumps and never knew it. I thought I was just getting yellow and fat."

"Which plays?" asked Lucy.

"Well, let's see," said Elliot. "First play was *Inherit the Wind*. I played the reporter."

"Gene Kelly did it in the movie," said Lucy. She turned her face up, placed the fork over her wide-open mouth, and unreeled the massive footage of spaghetti down her throat.

"Check," said Elliot. "Kelly did a nice job, but maybe didn't dig as deep as I did. Who knows? Then I did *Cyrano*."

Paula stared at the ceiling and shook her head. The hell with her, thought Elliot. She wants to crawl off in a corner, fine. Let her. We'll all be better off, Lucy included.

"Jose Ferrer," said Lucy. "I saw it last week on Channel nine."

"I used half the nose and got twice the laughs," said Elliot. "It's style that counts, not the make-up."

Lucy looked at him and smiled knowingly. "Tell me, when did you first realize you had an inferiority complex?"

"Hey!" said Elliot. "Atta girl. I see you got at least one good thing from your mother. That's a pretty hefty phrase for a little kid."

"Girl," said Lucy. "Kid means goat."

"Girl," corrected Elliot.

"You seem to think a lot of yourself," said Lucy.

Elliot nodded. "Pound for pound, I got the biggest ego this side of St. Louis. In this business, you better believe in yourself. Otherwise they'll chop you up and serve you for an onion dip."

He glanced over at Paula. No reaction. Blank stare. "What else?" he continued. "I was a disc jockey for a year. No good. You gotta see my face to appreciate the work."

He thought back to KRTW, the two-room Polish radio station where he and Eddie Wankowski, his engineer, would spend four hours a day working up material and eight hours broadcasting it. He'd tried to vary the old music-and-five-minute-news pattern by doing book reviews, consumer features, commentaries, and even, for a few months, a two-man soap opera. The people weren't buying. Advertising revenues plummeted disastrously.

"They want their polkas and their marching songs and a weather forecast," Wankowski had said. "Believe me, I know. I look at my parents. Don't give them mental stimulation."

"Who's stimulating?" Elliot had answered. "Soap opera is stimulating? It's just a little change, that's all."

"The only change they want is another record."

After eleven months, the station's owner, a man named Donahue, had fired them both. "I'm sorry," Elliot had apologized to Wankowski. "It was my fault. What can I say?" "You tried," Wankowski had said. "You had to try."

"Then I taught drama," Elliot told Lucy. "At Duluth Junior College. One semester."

"You taught drama?" said Lucy. "Far out!"

"Very far out," said Elliot. "Near Canada. On weekends there was nothing to do but ski and scr —*ski* some more. Half the faculty were popping small purple things in their mouths that made the time pass more quickly. You ever read *One Day in the Life of Ivan Denisovitch*?"

"No."

"Well, we didn't have to eat gruel, but the other similarities were too close for comfort. Anyway, I had twelve students, and I flunked seven of them."

"You were mean," said Lucy.

"No, no, not at all. I merely have very high standards. Needless to say, they canned me."

He looked again at Paula, who was still maintaining her ice-cold, stony stare. He picked up the Chianti bottle and held it out. "A little more wine?"

She did not answer, but gazed fixedly at her plate.

"Nienti on the Chianti," said Elliot, putting the bottle down.

"Hey, that's good," said Lucy. "You're terrific with words. You always pick the right ones."

Elliot thought for a moment. "Words are the canvas of the actor," he said, gesturing theatrically. "His lips are his brushes, and his tongue the colors of the spectrum. And when he speaks, he paints portraits . . ."

Lucy laughed. "Classy! You're very classy."

Elliot puffed himself up and turned to Paula. "The kid's got a good eye."

Paula didn't answer.

Why am I trying so hard to win her favor, thought Elliot. After all, he could have Rhonda any day or night of the week, a sweet, pliant, younger girl, better-looking, much nicer tits, probably much superior in bed. Undemanding. All right, maybe not as quick-witted as Paula was. Possibly less intelligent. But what the hell did that mean, anyway? The woman used her wit in the service of bitchiness and sullen ill-humor. The hell with her. *Then why did he keep playing to her*? He was even using Lucy, a really good kid, as a foil, a mirror to bounce words over to Paula. Because, thought Elliot, my "monumental" ego is as fragile as a pane of glass. I can't stand disapproval. Anyone's.

"You're not like Tony," said Lucy.

"Well," said Elliot. "Thanks. You don't bear much resemblance to Attila the Hun, either."

"He wasn't a classy actor," Lucy went on. "He was just, you know, sexy."

"And you don't find me sexy?" said Elliot.

Lucy giggled. "Are you kidding?"

"What do *you* know?" said Elliot. "You're ten

years old. In three years, I'll drive you out of your bird."

Paula threw down her napkin and stood up.

That got a rise out of the old girl, thought Elliot.

"Okay," said Paula. "It's after nine. Do your homework."

"I don't think I have any today," said Elliot.

Paula picked up her plate and Lucy's and headed for the sink, ignoring him.

"Five more minutes," Lucy told her. And then, to Elliot, "Talk more. We never have good talking like this at dinner."

"Then," said Elliot, "I did *Midsummer Night's Dream* on public television in Chicago." He watched her child's face, saw the unabashed, intense interest, the concentration, the mixture of total innocence and occasional sophistication. A pretty kid. Someone you'd like to have around as a niece . . . or daughter. "I did the part Mickey Rooney did in the movie." He pointed to her.

"Puck!" said Lucy, delighted with herself and with him.

"Right on! Then I got a call from this lady producer in New York who saw it, and she asked me to come and do *Richard the Third* off-Broadway. Well . . . off-off-off."

"Are we invited to the opening?" said Lucy, her eyes wide, a piece of spaghetti dangling to her chin.

Elliot cocked his head. "You really wanna come?" He looked toward the kitchen. "Both of you? Tuesday night."

"Tuesday night's a school night," intoned Paula from the sink, without turning around.

"We went to Tony's opening on a school night," whined Lucy.

"I said no," said Paula curtly.

106

"Ah, shit!" said Lucy. "Shoot, I mean. Sorry."

Paula glared at her.

Lucy stood up. "I think I'm in trouble. G'night." She carried her dishes to the sink, and then headed for her room.

Paula stood silently, while Elliot stared down at the table. Two minutes passed. Elliot sniffed.

"Would you be interested in my bedroom?" said Paula softly.

Elliot looked around. "What?"

"Would you be interested in my bedroom?"

"Are you talking to me?"

"You can have the big bedroom for an extra fifty dollars a month. Payable right now in cash. We'll move into yours in the morning."

"You mean," said Elliot slowly, "a rent increase for getting what I should have gotten what I didn't get in the first place? No, thank you. I don't want to whitewash your fence, either, if that's the next question."

"Would you be interested in *lending* me fifty dollars?" said Paula, swallowing hard. "I'll either pay you seven and a half percent interest or do your laundry. Take your pick."

Elliot nodded. A woman in distress. "They really cleaned you out, huh?"

"Everyone from here to Italy," said Paula.

This has got to be it, she thought. This instant, here and now, must be the low point of my life to date. Nothing, not when Lenny was suffocating me in the fraternity house, not when Bobby ran away, or even Tony, or even when those bastards yanked away my purse—nothing was worse than this moment. I grovel, thought Paula. Not for myself, because I'd sooner starve, but for Lucy. I do this for her.

Elliot had stood up and was removing money from his pocket. "I have . . . twenty-eight dollars and change." The woman must think I'm a beast, he thought. "I'll split it with you. And starting with opening night, I get two hundred and forty dollars a week. I'll make you an offer. I'll pay all the living expenses until you get yourself a job."

He watched her face carefully.

"And I'll do my own laundry," he added.

Paula nodded suspiciously. Who did he think he was dealing with? "I see," she said, in very neutral tones. "And what do *you* get?"

Elliot looked at her and said, very sincerely, "All you have to do is—be nice to me."

"You go to hell!" Paula exploded. See? she thought. See? Did that prove it, or did that prove it? The man was a dirt-turtle, an animal. She flung the scrubbing brush against the back of the sink and stormed into the living room.

Elliot followed and spoke deliberately to her back. "Would you listen very, very carefully, because this may be the last time I'm ever talking to you."

Good, thought Paula.

"Not everybody in this world is after your magnificent body, lady. In the first place, it ain't so magnificent. Fair, maybe, but it doesn't keep me up nights."

Paula pressed her lips together, but somehow, for some reason, began to feel less angry.

"I don't even find you that pretty," continued Elliot. "Maybe if you smiled once in a while, who knows? But I wouldn't want you to do anything against your religion." He moved closer to her and began to circle around so that he could talk to her face, but she caught sight of him in her peripheral vision and turned away.

"And you're not the only one in this city who got dumped on," said Elliot. "I, myself, am a recent dumpee. I am a dedicated actor, dedicated to my art and my craft." He felt like an orator. The mystery was why she continued to listen to him. "I value what I do. And because of a mentally arthritic director, I am playing the second greatest English-speaking role in history like a double order of fresh California fruit salad! When I say be nice to me, I mean *nice*."

Paula knew very well why she stood there and absorbed the abuse. She had made a mistake. A snap judgment based on her own lousy mood and pre-conditioned attitudes. And it was only correct now that she pay for it. The man was entitled to his say.

"Decent!" said Elliot. "That's what I mean by 'nice.' Fair! I deserve it because I am a nice, decent, fair person. I do *not* want to jump on your bones. I don't even want to *see* you when I get up in the morning." He paused, and then said more softly, "But I'll tell you what I do like about you."

Paula inhaled and turned to face him.

"Lucy," said Elliot. "Lucy is your best part." He slapped money down on the table. "There's fourteen dollars for the care and feeding of that terrific child. You get nothing."

Paula felt the water begin to come into her eyes. She parted her lips to speak, but nothing came out.

"You need money for yourself," said Elliot sternly, "borrow from Lucy. Okay?"

Paula nodded her head, almost imperceptibly.

Elliot felt drained. "I am now going inside to meditate away my hostility toward you. But personally, I don't think it can be done." He pivoted, walked briskly into his room, and slammed the door hard.

Paula stood there and looked after him.

It was nearly the end of the term, but Lucy's teacher still couldn't remember names. She was an old-timer, Mrs. Fanning, fond of shawls and shoes with laces, and when she wanted to address a member of the class, she simply called "Boy!" or "Girl!" as the case might be, or "Child!" if she wasn't sure. The fact was that teaching had become too much for her, and what she really wanted was to retire. Since she couldn't afford to actually retire, she did the next best thing—nothing. Over her forty-one-year career she'd accumulated thousands of ditto-sheet exercises; two of these in the morning, and two in the afternoon, kept the children away. Like headaches. There was a math ditto and a reading ditto, and a science ditto and a history ditto. Simple. The pledge of allegiance. Ditto. Ditto. Send them off to music. Lunch. Ditto. Send them off to art. Recess. Ditto. And home. It was a progressive school. The classrooms had TV sets. Mrs. Fanning's class, which included Lucy McFadden, often got to watch *Casper the Ghost*, which Mrs. Fanning didn't mind as long as they were quiet and didn't bother her. One of her pupils, one of the three whose names she knew, even had a personal assignment: to watch and tell Mrs. Fanning if the water was boiling for her tea.

It was twenty to three, and Lucy whispered over to her friend, Cynthia Fein, "Did you finish your unit yet?"

"What unit? You mean on Venezuela? That one?"

"Is that yours?"

Mrs. Fanning had organized the class into groups, each of which had to produce reports on different foreign countries. When they were done, each of the groups read the reports aloud, thus theoretically exchanging information, at minimal cost to the teacher.

"Yes," said Cynthia Fein. "Only they don't seem to do anything down there. Oil and iron ore is all we could find, and that only uses half a page."

"Same here," said Lucy. "We got Nova Scotia."

"And Steven Melman doesn't contribute," said Cynthia. "He spends the whole day cutting into his desk with that pocket kni—"

"You!" said Mrs. Fanning, from the front of the room. "You, girl! You stop talking now."

Cynthia bent her head down immediately, as did Lucy. After a minute, when Mrs. Fanning appeared to look away, Cynthia said, "How's Elliot?"

Lucy winked. "Not bad. He was real angry last night, though."

"Angry at you?"

"Nah. My mom."

"Why?"

"I'm not sure, really. I couldn't hear that well. It sounded like he was being nice to her, and then he wanted her to be nice also."

"So?"

"So, she didn't want to," said Lucy.

"But why? You say he's a groove."

"I don't know," said Lucy. "My mother's pretty cranky sometimes."

At three o'clock the bell rang. Mrs. Fanning stopped them both on their way out. "Each of you girls, for tomorrow, will write five hundred times 'I must not talk in class.' Is there any question why I've selected you two?"

The girls shook their heads.

"Good," said Mrs. Fanning.

They walked out of the classroom.

"My mother's gonna kill me when she hears this," said Cynthia.

"Do like I do," said Lucy. "Don't tell her."

As they walked down the steps in front of the school, a cab pulled up to the curb. Paula leaned out of the window.

"Lucy! Lucy!"

"Excuse me," said Lucy. "That's my mother." This is either very good or very bad, she thought, as she ran to the taxi.

"Get in!" said Paula.

"What are you doing in a taxi?" asked Lucy. For a crazy instant she had an impression that her mother might be pregnant and somehow having an emergency.

"Will you get in?" repeated Paula.

She opened the door and yanked Lucy into the cab. "What is this, a kidnapping?" said the driver.

"Name something you want!" Paula told Lucy exuberantly.

"Are you pregnant?"

"What? Come on. Just name something. Anything."

"My own cab," said the driver.

"A dress. A coat," continued Paula, ignoring him. "Earrings, bracelets, whatever. You name it."

Lucy was still suspicious. "You mean I get one wish?"

"And don't take all day," said Paula. "The cab driver's gonna get half your wish."

"Ask for two cabs," muttered the driver.

Lucy thought. "I'll have the lichee duck at Sun Ming's," she said finally.

"No craziness," said Paula. "You have to pick something normal."

"Oh, Mom."

"Normal."

"Uhhh . . . Okay. Then, the biggest chocolate dessert at Serendipity."

"That's it?" said Paula. "You blew leather boots for that?"

"What should *I* say?" said the driver.

They sat in the back room, and glanced occasionally at the stained-glass colored ceiling. Lucy had ordered a giant hot fudge sundae; Paula, a small bottle of white wine.

"So what kind of show is it?" asked Lucy, her speech muffled under the avalanche of warm, molten chocolate, frothy whipped topping, crunchy almonds, and the almost obscured vanilla ice cream. "A muzh . . . musical?"

"It's not a *show* show," said Paula. "It's an auto show."

"I never heard of that," said Lucy, patting her stomach.

"They show off their new cars. And I stand on this slow moving turntable with this cute little sports car."

"Where is this?"

"In the Coliseum."

"You mean, you help people show off their cars?"

"I get to wear this really all-American outfit, too," said Paula. "Blue blazer, white skirt, and a red blouse."

"What kind of car?"

"A Subaru."

"Never heard of it."

"It's Japanese."

"So why do you dress all-American?"

"Because I don't look good in all-Japanese," said Paula. "Anyway, I stand there and I say— where's that sheet?"

"You say 'Where's that sheet?' "

"Don't be wise," said Paula, fumbling in her bag, an old black one that had once belonged to her mother. It was the only one she had left after the robbery. She finally found the sheet of paper, removed it, and began to read.

"With the SEEC-T engine, Subaru models recorded an improvement of nineteen point five percent in economy over their nineteen-seventy-five record."

Lucy dug the long spoon down to the bottom of her glass. "Sounds like an exciting show," she said sarcastically.

Paula caught the tone. "Four hundred dollars a week for two weeks sounds *plenty* exciting. Especially to the check-out girl at Finast."

"I don't feel too good," said Lucy, holding her chest.

"Really?" said Paula.

Lucy shook her head.

"Maybe you shouldn't eat any more."

"That's what I said after the first one," said Lucy. Her stomach made gurgling noises.

Paula leaned over. "I'm sorry, baby. I just wanted to treat you to something special. It's been so long. . . ."

Lucy was holding her stomach. "I should have picked the boots."

They walked home with Paula holding Lucy up, stopping every five or six paces.

"One second," Lucy would say, "I think I want to double over for a little while."

114

And they'd wait until the pain would pass and then go on.

"I can't believe this is just from the ice cream," said Paula. "Something must've been brewing there a long time. Maybe some of your sardines were contaminated, or something."

"I don't know," said Lucy haltingly. "But whatever was brewing seems to be ready now."

"Just one more block," said Paula. "You have to go number two?"

"I already did, twice."

"Is it your stomach that hurts?"

Lucy shook her head yes. "And chest," she added. She retched, but nothing came up.

Paula wished it were she, instead of her daughter. She remembered, years ago, how one night she began vomiting uncontrollably, and after nine or ten times, when all that was left was the dry heaves, Bobby had hailed a cab and taken her to the emergency room at Bellevue. They'd waited for nearly two hours while people whose heads were gushing blood, who were choking, whose arms or legs were dangling by threads, were attended to first. Finally, an Indian doctor had examined her and given her a spoonful of green liquid.

"This will make the insides calm," he'd said, in a clipped, reedy voice.

Later, they'd taken a taxi back home, and Paula had retched in the street just as they got out. "Anything come up?" Bobby had asked.

"Just the calming green liquid," said Paula.

Now when she finally got Lucy upstairs, she gave her a sedative and put her right to bed, not even bothering to remove her clothes.

"Lie on your side and try to get to sleep," said Paula. "It's the best thing for you."

115

If she's still sick tomorrow, I can't leave her to go to my job. The hell with it, thought Paula–All that money'll ruin the shape of my pocketbook, anyway.

Chapter 8

Elliot sat cross-legged on the bed with his script. It was interesting—in a very simple, straightforward way, he had managed to pilot his life at seventy miles an hour directly into a bridge abutment. To continue with this *Richard III* was to move forward to certain critical disaster. To quit, however, was to unthinkably screw everyone else in the company and generate enough bad publicity to insure not working for a good long time. He was caught, with no way of escape. He shifted on the bed and felt his jeans tear slightly at the crotch, just as someone knocked on the door.

"What is it?" He stood up, crossed the room, and opened the door.

"Am I disturbing you?" said Paula. Her eyes looked large; her voice was soft.

"Yes," said Elliot.

"I'm sorry," said Paula.

"Then don't disturb me," said Elliot quickly.

"You don't have to snap at me."

"That wasn't snapping," corrected Elliot. "That was sarcasm. Snapping is, 'Bug off, I'm busy,' or the equivalent. You see the difference?"

Paula noticed that his voice seemed a bit higher

than usual, his words faster. The easy confidence seemed gone. She said, "What's wrong?"

He slouched against the doorway. "What's wrong, she asks. *You* open tomorrow night in front of the New York critics wearing a chartreuse hump on your back."

Paula held her lower lip under her top teeth. It would be bad form to laugh.

"*You* play Richard with a twisted paralytic hand and pink polish on your nails," continued Elliot. He wondered vaguely if the tear in his crotch was noticeable. Why did this woman always seem to pop up at inopportune times? "You want to know what's wrong, I'll tell you what's wrong. I'm busy trying to figure out how to save my goddamn career from going down the toilet bowl, that's what's wrong."

"Oh," said Paula.

"What is it exactly that *you* want?" said Elliot. "Oh, wait, I know. I dipped into your peanut butter, is that it? The alarm must've gone off, and an assistant district attorney is on the way right now to give me a summons. Is that it? Well, I'll pay, I'll pay! Call off the suit. What do I owe you for one finger full of Skippy Chunky spread?"

Paula was not in the least bit angry. "I came to pay you back your fourteen dollars," she said. She took the bills, which she'd had ready, lifted his hand, and pressed them into his palm.

"Oh. Uh, look, I—"

"I got a job," she went on. "Also I want to know if you have some bicarbonate. I ran out, and Lucy is sick."

"What's wrong with her?" said Elliot.

"I'm not sure," said Paula. "She had two double hot fudge sundaes, and then it started. It was my fault. I'm a terrible mother, I let her have them."

Elliot glared at her. "Incredible! Really incredible."

"She's had them before," Paula said defensively. "Although maybe not two in a row. But still. . . ."

"I don't know why they don't sell insurance policies to kids," said Elliot. He walked back into his room, grabbed his guitar, and stormed past Paula to Lucy's bedroom.

"Is that bicarbonate?" called Paula to his back.

Lucy was bunched in a fetal ball, rocking and moaning. She still had on the jeans she'd worn to school. Elliot came in and sat down on the side of the bed. Paula followed.

"Lucy," said Elliot softly.

Lucy grunted.

"Lucy, can you hear me?"

"The problem isn't in her ears," said Paula.

"How's it feel, Lucy?" said Elliot.

"Did you see *The Exorcist*?" said Lucy weakly.

"Yes."

"Well, you better get out of the room."

"Look," said Elliot, "she has a sense of humor even in her sickness. Listen, Lucy, try to just . . . relax."

Paula looked at the ceiling. *You ask for bicarbonate, this is what you get. Relax.*

"Come on," said Elliot, grasping Lucy's feet and trying to straighten her out. "See if you can turn. You want to try turning? See if you can turn on your back."

Lucy remained as she was, stiff and shivering.

"Don't you trust me?" said Elliot.

"I trusted my mother today," said Lucy, "and look how I feel."

Elliot shot a glance toward Paula, then turned back. "Come on, you have to give it a try. The more tense you are, the worse it's going to hurt. Turn—come on—okay—that's it. Good. Good. Flat on your back, that's it. Okay, deep breaths, now. Slow, slow, deep breaths now." He inhaled and exhaled several times in illustration. He turned to Paula. "Come here."

Paula came over to the bed. Elliot motioned for her to sit on the other side. "Watch this," he whispered.

With the flat palm of his hand, he began making gentle, soothing circles on Lucy's stomach.

A medicine man, thought Paula. Any minute he'll go into his dance.

"There we go," said Elliot soothingly. "There we go now." He looked toward Paula. "You think you can do that?"

"I might be able to manage it," she said.

She put her palm on Lucy's stomach and made a few tentative rotary motions. Elliot took her hand and moved it in wider, firmer circles. His touch was warm and reassuring.

"You got it?" he said.

Paula nodded.

Elliot reached for his guitar. "Don't stop. Lucy, eyes closed. You hear? Deep breaths now. Remember, I showed you? Okay. Deep breaths."

He leaned back against the bedpost and began, softly, to play the guitar. Paula tried to time her revolutions to the rhythm. The man is crazy, she thought. He thinks he's the village healer. Next, I'll have to get the roots of an eggplant and the brains of a bat for him. Lucy moaned softly as Paula kept rubbing and Elliot played. Gradually,

Lucy began to relax. Her hands, which had been balled into tight fists, unclenched.

"How's it feel?" said Elliot, continuing to strum.

Lucy nodded. "A little better."

"Isn't this more soothing than some medicine?" said Elliot.

"And it tastes better, too," said Lucy. Her eyes began to brighten.

Maybe the two of them dreamed this up, thought Paula. Just to impress me.

"How's the play going?" said Lucy.

"Please," said Elliot, stroking the strings in a deliberate downthrust, "one sick person at a time."

Lucy yawned. Her words came slowly. "Sure wish we could go to the opening. . . ."

Elliot looked at Paula. A dramatic show, she thought, for my benefit.

"Mom?" said Lucy.

"What, baby?"

"Could we? I mean, you said 'one wish' today."

"But you had that."

"You're gonna count this? Today was the pits."

"All right," said Paula. "Anything you say."

Lucy closed her eyes. "That's terrific." Her breathing grew regular. "Now you have to get me a . . . ." Her mouth fell open.

Paula kept up the circles on her stomach for another three minutes, then stopped. Lucy was fast asleep. Elliot continued his strumming.

"Thank you," Paula whispered.

Elliot did not look up. She arose and walked to a corner of the room. Keeping her back turned, she said, very clearly, "I'm sorry about yesterday."

There was no answer, other than a slightly atonal chord.

"That was very generous of you," said Paula.

121

The words, tumbling out of her, felt right, correct. "I'm not used to the kindness of strangers. I know, don't say it—Blanche DuBois in *Streetcar*. Sometimes I feel just like her. Every time you trust a man, they take you away at the end of the movie." She felt the maudlin, gushy self-pity that usually preceded tears. She held back, determined this time not to concede. "Anyway, I'm sorry for—well, I'm just sorry."

The guitar stopped, but she did not turn.

"If you're listening," she said, "that's my attempt to be nice, decent, and fair. How am I doing?"

No answer. Paula whirled around. Half-leaning, half-slumped, Elliot had fallen asleep, his head lolling peacefully over his guitar. Paula crossed to him.

"Mr. Garfield?"

She touched his shoulder, and the light push was sufficient to tip him over sideways, landing him next to Lucy, the guitar over his chest.

"Mr. Garfield?" Paula shook him, to no avail. "Mr. Garfield, you can't sleep with my daughter."

She was afraid to shout for fear of awakening Lucy. "Mr. Garfield," she whispered urgently.

No response. He was either totally, deeply asleep, or doing an expert fake.

Paula stood thinking for a few moments, then turned off the light and left the room. She had a fleeting notion to go to sleep in Elliot's bed, but then thought: What if, in the middle of the night, he decides to return to his own room? By his own words, he possessed no pajamas. It would be just like him to flop into bed completely naked. . . . She decided to sleep on the living room couch. She removed the rear pillows to give herself some more space, then kicked off her slippers and lay down.

Imagine, the two of them, sleeping in there. Everyone but me, thought Paula. Everyone but me.

She awoke the next morning to the sound of soft chanting coming from the kitchen.

"Om mommanomma, om mommanomma, om mommanomma, ommmm."

Paula rose from the couch and stretched, then walked through the kitchen door and sat down at the table.

"Morning," she said to Elliot, who'd apparently just finished his ritual.

"Well," said Elliot. "Morning. How's everything? How's Lucy?"

"Don't know," said Paula. "I just got up."

"She was sleeping fine early this morning," said Elliot.

"I'll check," said Paula.

She tiptoed into Lucy's room. "Baby?" she said softly.

Lucy stirred. "Ma?"

"Yes. You awake?"

"Uh-huh. Where's Elliot?"

"In the kitchen. How do you feel?"

"Well . . . better than yesterday."

"But something still hurts you?" She touched Lucy's forehead. It felt cool.

"Not really. Maybe my stomach, a little."

"All right," said Paula. "Look, we can't take chances. You might have a virus. You'll stay home today from school. If you feel better, you'll go in tomorrow."

Lucy thought, Now I don't have to write five hundred times *I must not talk in class.* Everything had worked out for the best. Poor Cynthia. "But what about your job?" she asked.

"I'll call in sick," said Paula. "Today was only a

123

little dry run, anyway. The show doesn't start till tomorrow. You rest now."

She returned to the kitchen. "She seems a little under the weather," she told Elliot, who was spooning some health food mixture from a bowl. "She's better, but I think I'll keep her home just for today."

"Seems reasonable," said Elliot.

Paula began cooking herself an egg. "I want to thank you for what you—"

"Nope. Say no more," said Elliot. "My pleasure. I'd even do the same for you. Sorry I forced you to vacate your bed last night, that's all."

"It's all right," said Paula, watching her egg cook. "Now if I can just get up the guts to call in sick, my day will be complete."

"You want *me* to?" said Elliot.

"What?"

"Call in for you?"

"You can't—. Well, I don't . . . uh . . . Would you?"

"Sure."

"Jesus, it would be a lot easier. I always find it hard to *sound* sick, you know."

"No problem," said Elliot. He rose and walked to the phone. "What's the number?"

"Oh. Wait a minute. See that paper by the side of the phone? Near the top. You see there's a number? That's it."

Elliot dialed. "Who do I ask for?"

"Mr. Ishiburo."

"Who?"

"Ishiburo. They're Japanese."

Elliot nodded. He heard two rings, and then a female voice answered. "Mr. Ishiburo, please," said Elliot firmly.

Paula leaned back. *I wonder if he'll say he's my husband.*

"Hello?" said Elliot. "Mr. Ishiburo? Yes. This is Doctor Garfield, Paula McFadden's physician."

"Who?" said Ishiburo.

"McFadden. One of the models for the show?"

"Ah, the show. Yes?"

"Well, she won't be in today. I've been treating her for a sub-inguinal blastosis, and I've recommended she spend the day in bed. She should be completely recovered by tomorrow."

"Ah. Yes. I see. Thank you, Doctor. We see her tomollow."

Elliot hung up, and Paula laughed. "Doctor Garfield. Terrific," she said.

"I believe what you've just seen will top any performance I can give tonight," said Elliot. "You are coming, aren't you? I have two tickets for you."

She stared at him. "Provided my sub-inguinal blastosis clears up," she said. "And provided Lucy is better."

"Lucy will be better," said Elliot confidently. "That, I guarantee. About the other thing, just keep away from beets."

"I never eat beets."

Elliot smiled sweetly. "Then I foresee no problems."

As usual, he was physically shaking. It always happened before he went on, and most times it really didn't feel that bad. Most times he was nervous, yet confident, not scared. Tonight, however, he was nervous *and* scared. Tonight he was marking the end of a career that had never begun. From the wings, he peeked out into the audience. He could see the critics seated in the first row, studying their

125

programs and chatting. He recognized Clive Barnes and Richard Watts. He scanned the audience, trying unsuccessfully to spot Paula and Lucy. The theater was three-quarters full. Maybe they weren't here yet. He felt a hand on his shoulder and turned.

"You're shaking," said Rhonda.

"Just exercising my skin," said Elliot.

"It's going to work fine," said Rhonda.

"Oh, sure," said Elliot. "I know. Mark knows what he's doing." He paused. "You believe that?"

"You know me, Elliot. I believe anything."

The house lights darkened.

Near the rear of the theater, Paula and Lucy made their way to their seats. A number of people in their row stood up to let them pass.

"Excuse me." "Sorry." "Pardon me."

They sat down and opened their programs.

"I'm glad it didn't start yet," said Lucy. "I hope this is going to be funny. Is it a comedy?"

"It's Shakespeare," said Paula.

Lucy closed her program. "Booor-ing!"

"Shh!"

A spotlight suddenly illuminated center stage, and Paula inhaled involuntarily.

Elliot as Richard. He limped a few steps, then stopped. He was both twisted and humped, and his costume shone bright chartreuse. He smiled be-guilingly at the audience, letting his eyebrows rise, and his gaze sweep from side to side. He pursed his lips.

"Now is the winter of our discontent
Made glorious summer by this son of York

126

And all the clouds that lowered upon our house
In the deep bosom of the ocean buried."

Already, I begin to die, he thought.

In the audience, mouths—including Lucy's—
dropped open. Paula lowered her eyes. *The poor
man.*

"He sounds like that guy in the beauty parlor,
what's his name?"

"Mr. Bernie," said Paula.

"Yeah, him."

"He sounds worse," said Paula.

Elliot continued, trying to speed up the delivery.

"Now are our brows bound with victorious wreaths,
Our bruised arms hung up for monuments,
Our stern alarums changed to merry meetings,
Our dreadful marches to delightful measures."

It went on, interminably. Even before the first act
ended, Elliot could feel the audience stirring, sense
the movement in the seats out there.

He was waiting offstage with the actor who played
Ratcliffe when Mark Bodine flashed past.

"Terrific," Mark whispered loudly. "Spectacular."

"Hear that?" said Elliot. "I'm a spectacle." Then
he caught his cue, and limped out on stage,

"Good morrow to my sovereign king and queen;
And, princely peers, a happy time of day!"

The time passed in dreamlike, distorted spurts.
He mouthed the lines mechanically, scarcely conscious of what he was saying. He shook his head
once, as if to clear it, and found himself in the

middle of act three, scene five. He wore tight fuchsia trousers—when had he changed?—and an écru top. On stage, the actors who played Lovel and Ratcliffe held a tray with a towel-covered cantaloupe that simulated Hastings's head.

"Be patient," said Elliot, "they are friends—Ratcliffe and Lovel."

"Here is the head of that ignoble traitor," said Lovel. "The dangerous and unsuspected Hastings."

Elliot lifted the towel and glanced at the canteloupe. He felt the perspiration on his forehead as he spoke.

"So dear I loved the man that I must weep:
I took him for the plainest harmless creature
That breathed upon the earth a Christian;
Make him my book—"

In the audience, the man next to Lucy rose and began to move sideways.

"Excuse me, please. 'Scuse."

Lucy, who'd begun to nod off, looked up suddenly. "Is it over? Is the play over yet?"

"It is for me," said the man.

Lucy looked around. Almost a third of the original audience had left. "Where is everybody?" she said to Paula.

Paula looked at her watch. "A lot of people leave plays early," she said. "They have work the next day." She paused. "Which reminds me. Did you have homework? I hope you did it."

"I can't seem to remember," said Lucy, struggling to keep her eyes open. On stage, trumpets sounded and drums rolled, but even these couldn't keep her awake. She dozed, her head on Paula's shoulder. When she next snapped to consciousness, she caught the last line of a speech by Catesby.

"Rescue, fair lord, or else the day is lost!"

Elliot limped back on stage, his uniform in very neat, impossibly colorful rags.

"A horse! A horse! My kingdom for a horse!"

A man stood up in the first row. "That's what I'd give for a taxi," he said irritably to a friend, and he walked out. Those in the audience who heard chuckled loudly.

Finally, mercifully, the play ended. The cast, one by one, came out for final bows. Elliot emerged last. The applause, except for Lucy's, was polite, but perfunctory. Then Paula and Lucy rose with the rest of the audience.

"Weird city," said Lucy.

"Shh," said Paula. "Someone will hear you."

"Someone already said it," said Lucy. "That's where I got it. Can we go backstage and say hello?"

"I . . . have a feeling he'd rather be alone," said Paula.

"Seems to me he'll know we thought it was lousy if we don't go back."

"All right," said Paula. "But try to be tactful."

"What's tactful?"

"Lie," said Paula.

They made their way backstage and got to the dressing rooms. Actually, they weren't rooms, but cubicles. Actually, they weren't even cubicles, but sort of cordoned-off areas, separated and shielded from each other by bedsheets supported by a network of ropes. Actors and visitors milled about

129

outside. Mark Bodine walked jauntily through the crowd, clasping hands, thanking people who hadn't addressed him, finally stopping at a middle-aged woman.

"Wonderful job, Mark," said the woman without enthusiasm.

Bodine's face lit up. "Did you really love it? I mean really, *really* love it?"

"It was"—the woman hesitated—"interesting. Quite interesting."

"Oh, God!" Mark shouted. "Hey, everybody"— people looked around—"my mother loved it! My mother loved it, everybody!"

He kissed the woman grandly on the lips and continued to move through the crowd. A teenage girl grabbed his arm. "Are you the director?"

"Yes."

"Well, my question is, wouldn't a non-linear interpretation be more organic to the play's construction than the perspective you selected?"

"Quite possibly," said Bodine, wiping lazily at his forehead. "I saw it from backstage."

He sauntered off, passing Paula and Lucy, and kissing Paula lightly on the cheek.

"Thank you," he said effusively. "We're all very excited. And it couldn't have happened without your support." He patted Lucy on the head, and moved on.

"He must've thought I was someone else," said Paula.

She took Lucy's hand and made her way over to a sheet that had "Elliot Garfield" pinned on it. She raised her hand to knock, then lowered it. "Hello?" she called.

No answer.

"Hello-oh? Hello? Mr. Garfield? It's Lucy and Paula. Hello?"

They waited a moment, and finally the sheet was pulled back. Elliot stood there half naked, his body bare to the waist. He looked as if he were about to cry. A tiny, barely perceptible smile flickered across his lips, then collapsed.

"I had the best time," said Lucy.

Elliot nodded somberly.

"At first I thought it would be boring," said Lucy. "But then it picked up near the end."

Elliot said nothing.

"Okay, Lucy," said Paula. She looked at Elliot. "We won't keep you. We just wanted to thank you for the tickets, and for a lovely evening."

Elliot nodded, looking down.

"People were talking about you on the way out," said Lucy, with too much brightness. "They wanted to remember your name, so they'll know who to look for next time."

Paula put her hand under Lucy's elbow, and exerted firm, pulling pressure. "*Come on*, Lucy. Good night, Mr. Garfield."

Elliot looked at them glassily and nodded again. He was unable to speak. He closed the sheet and sat down in his chair. Outside, not far away enough for him not to hear, Lucy said, "Well, it's not *his* fault. It's just a lousy play."

Chapter 9

After twenty minutes, with nearly everyone gone, Rhonda came into his cubicle. Elliot had finished dressing. He stood looking at the ceiling.

"Mark is having a little party at his apartment," Rhonda said. "I guess you're not going, huh?"

"No," said Elliot.

"Would you like to go out for some coffee?"

Elliot shook his head. "I don't think so."

She moved around behind him, and began to massage his shoulders. "How's the back?"

"What? Oh. Fine. Good. You did a terrific job on it that night." He patted her hand.

"Would you like to come up to my place for coffee? I could do the same job again."

Elliot stared down and patted her hand. "Rhonda, you're a beautiful, delightful girl, and that's the best offer anyone's made me in years." He closed his eyes. "But tonight's a really bad night for me." And for you too, he thought. *Don't you understand?* "I don't think I'm going to be good company tonight."

Rhonda inhaled and moved away. "Elliot, it's not the end of the world. It wasn't your performance that was bad, it was Mark's conception."

"The critics won't make the distinction."

"It's still just one play."

She was only making him feel worse for her failure to understand the magnitude of his disgrace.

"Rhonda—"

"Okay, okay. Listen, I understand."

She walked back to him and kissed him lightly on the cheek. "You have my number, El. Just call, if there's anything I can do to make you feel better. Otherwise, see you tomorrow." She strode to the door.

"Rhonda—" She stopped. "You're . . . a fine person. A really nice person."

She smiled and left the cubicle.

Elliot took a subway to Times Square, walked aimlessly for about forty minutes, and then went into a bar on 53rd Street. A rock band was blaring inhumanly loud music, and couples gyrated in a dizzying variety of dance styles on a small floor. People were jammed in at tables, and everywhere else you looked. Elliot pushed his way through to the bar. There were no unoccupied seats and he had to stand. Colored strobe lights blinked wildly in time to the music. Elliot could feel the drums in his chest. It took only a moment before the bartender was staring at him. A hawk-faced man with a big nose.

"Yeah."

"Scotch rocks," Elliot said. "And keep them coming. If the glass looks empty, fill it."

The bartender produced a bottle and poured the amber liquid into a glass.

"One-sixty. You pay as you go."

"Very sensible," said Elliot, reaching for his wallet.

After his third drink, he got a seat. After his fifth, a woman sat down next to him. Frizzy hair, lips a bit too thick, very short, tight skirt, and high heels.

"Hi," she said.

Elliot nodded.

"How're you t'night?"

"Wonderful," said Elliot. "I feel like I'm beginning a new life."

The woman smiled. "If you feel good now, I can make you feel better."

"Really?" said Elliot, signaling the bartender for a refill. He could feel his cheekbones begin to numb.

"Yes." The woman leaned closer. "I'm a lady of pleasure." She laughed wildly.

"I'm an actor," said Elliot. "I mean *was*."

"For a small consideration," said the woman, "you can have my company."

"I didn't know you owned a company," said Elliot groggily. "Actually, I'm not too interested in companies right now. I prefer the offshore funds." He giggled.

The woman tightened her lips and slid down off her seat. "S'long, creep."

"*Au revoir, ma chère*," said Elliot.

Paula and Lucy were fast asleep. Paula was dreaming she was in a large department store, talking to a good-looking male salesman behind the perfume counter.

"Isn't it rather unusual," she was saying, "a man to—"

Crash! Someone must've knocked something off a shelf, she dream-thought.

"Hey, what was that?" said the salesman in a voice that had suddenly turned feminine and childish.

Paula quickly sat up and found Lucy sitting next to her.

"What was that?" repeated Lucy.

"I don't know."

A second crash came from the living room, a heavier, duller sound. Paula got up, and put on her robe, and went to the door. "If I'm not back in ten minutes, come in with guns blazing."

The living room was dark. She tiptoed over to the light switch, inhaled, then pressed down and illuminated the room. She spotted a broken vase on the floor, then an overturned chair with Elliot sprawled alongside it. He grinned.

"Thou has brokenst thy vase," he said. "Thou owes thee twelve-ninety-five plus taxeth."

"Are you all right?" said Paula.

"Not according to the *Times*," said Elliot. "Have you read the *Times*?"

"You want some coffee?" said Paula. She wanted to go over and help him up, but was unsure how he'd react.

Elliot pulled a crumpled *Times* page from his pocket and scrutinized it very carefully, holding it close to his eyes. Finally, he began to read: "Elliot Garfield researched Richard the Third and discovered he was England's first badly dressed interior decorator." He laughed uproariously. "Oh, Jesus! Jesus, that's good. That's *tasty* writing."

Paula walked over, raised the overturned chair, and knelt to pick up pieces of the broken vase. Elliot sat up and removed a can of beer from his coat pocket. He opened it and some spritzed on the carpet.

"Hey!" said Paula.

"Sorry." He put the can to his lips and drank.

"I never pay attention to critics," said Paula.

"Good," said Elliot. "Then *you* go on tomorrow night." He giggled moronically. "The *News*. You want to hear what they said in the *News*?"

"Look, you don't—"

"I'll tell you. Quote. 'It never occurred to us that William Shakespeare wrote *The Wizard of Oz*. However, Elliot Garfield made a splendid Wicked Witch of the North.' Tacky. That's a tacky review. If you're going to kill me, do it with panache. You hear that? Panache. I hate that word."

"Mr. Garfield—"

"You know why? It's a phony word. It reminds me of spinach."

"I'm sorry," said Paula.

"Oh, what the hell," said Elliot. He rose, stumbled, and sank again to his knees. "It was just a silly little New York debut."

"There'll be others, I'm sure," said Paula.

"Ames, Iowa, is where it really counts. If you don't make it in Ames, you have career trouble."

He stood up and tottered uncertainly toward his bedroom. Paula watched in silence as he disappeared behind the door. A moment later he was back out.

"Channel five at least was honest," he said. "They put it on right after the sports. Some sour-faced guy with glasses."

"Stu Klein."

"Direct and honest, although not too imaginative. '*Richard the Third* stank,' he said. 'And Elliot Garfield was the stink*ee*.'"

He lurched back into his room. A moment later Paula heard a thud, and then a groan. She rushed inside and saw Elliot sprawled on the floor.

"Am I in bed?" he said.

Paula knelt down.

"Very firm mattress you have here," he said. "This a Sealy, or a Simmons?"

She put her arms under his and helped him to his feet. He smelled of alcohol.

"I thought you didn't put unhealthy things into your body," she said.

"I didn't," said Elliot. "I put it into Richard's. I'm trying to kill the son of a bitch."

He sat on the bed.

"Why don't you get some sleep?" said Paula.

"Oh," said Elliot. "Thank you for your concern."

"I'm also looking out for the furniture," said Paula. "It's not mine."

"You probably think I'm discouraged," said Elliot.

"Oh, no," said Paula. "Why?"

"You think I'm defeated, maybe. Upset. Just because of fourteen unimportant negative reviews."

Paula shook her head.

"Well, you bet your ass I am, baby," continued Elliot. "Whoops! Sorry. This apartment is PG, I keep forgetting. You bet your panache I'm upset, is what I meant."

He stood up again, tripped over nothing, and braced himself against a wall. Paula quickly removed his guitar from his path as he lurched toward the door.

"Not the living room," she said hastily. "Listen, the room wasn't designed for staggering, everything breaks there. Listen"—she searched for the right words—"you really were wonderful tonight, really. I know something about acting, and you were good, I'm telling you."

Elliot stumbled out into the living room.

Guess those weren't the right words, thought Paula, following.

"What do you mean, 'wonderful'?" said Elliot. "Don't bullshi—panache me, lady. I was an Elizabethan fruit fly. The Betty Boop of Stratford-on-Avon. I was putrid. Capital P, capital U, capital . . . uh, what . . . uh—"

"Capital T," said Paula, regretting it instantly.

"Capital trid," said Elliot. "Well, wasn't I? Hah? Hah?"

"It was an interesting interpretation."

"It was BULLSHIT! You didn't see their faces when I walked out on the stage? Two hundred and ten people all given a shot of Novocain? I want the truth!"

With surprising speed, he sidled over to another vase and held it over his head. "The truth, you hear! You tell me, or I'll smash this priceless antique nine-dollar Klein's vase to pieces. WAS I PUTRID OR NOT? SAY IT! SAY THAT WORD!"

Paula was frightened. Her next words were whispered. "Yes, you were putrid."

Elliot closed his eyes. "Jee-sus!" he yelled. Then, lower, "Jesus. You didn't have to tell me so bluntly."

"I'm sorry. Put the vase down, please."

Elliot lowered it, and she walked over and took it from him.

"I had a good moment here and there," he said plaintively. "Didn't I? My entrances were good. You could hear me." His voice grew weak. "Some of them you can't even hear." He fell onto a sofa.

"You sure I can't get you something?" said Paula. "Some of your health foods, maybe?"

"Don't walk out on me," said Elliot, his eyes suddenly focusing on her intently. "Once a night is enough."

"I'm here," said Paula. "I'm listening."

"I really can play that part, you know. I can play the hump off that guy. I was better on the bus coming from Chicago than I was on that stage tonight." He shook his head and blinked several times. "Now is the winter of our discontent," he began seriously, no lisp or prissiness evident in his voice. "Made glorious summer by this sun of York. And all the clouds that lowered upon our house. In the deep bosom of the ocean buried. Et cetera, et cetera, et cetera."

"That *is* good," said Paula. She thought: Jesus, they really did ruin him tonight. They castrated him. "It's wonderful. Honestly. It is."

"Thank you," said Elliot. "You're really not such a bad person, you know."

"I know."

"But that 'putrid' remark really hurt. Really got to me, you know."

"I know. I'm sorry, I don't know what came over me. I must've been thinking of something else. Anyway . . . good night."

She walked over to the switch and turned out the light.

"Don't tell Lucy what it said in the *Times*," called Elliot sleepily.

"I won't."

"Or the *News*."

"No."

"Or Channel two, four, five, seven, nine, and eleven. Anybody watch nine and eleven here? What do they have?"

"Oh, *Star Trek* reruns, I think," said Paula. "Bowling. Met games. Ghosts are popular. CB interference."

"Thank you," said Elliot. "Listen, uh . . . if anyone asks, I'm not giving autographs right now, okay?"

"I understand," said Paula.

She had an impulse to go over and kiss him gently on the forehead. Instead, she returned to her bedroom. She thought about him living here, thought about herself, Lucy. . . . She took off her robe and lay down in bed. His failure, her audition. . . . And suddenly she burst into tears, lots of them. They streamed down her cheeks in droves, an army of salty droplets. She buried her head in the pillow.

"What's wrong?" asked Lucy.

"Nothing."

"So why are you crying?"

"I didn't cry today. Do you mind?" Her face was swollen.

Lucy shrugged. "No." She turned back over on her side. "I didn't think he was *that* bad."

Lucy ate a pizza and read the *Times*, while Paula braided her hair. Outside, the morning sun shone bright and clean in a cloudless sky.

" 'One must always respect brave and courageous attempts,' " read Lucy aloud, " 'to explore Shakespeare through new and daring concepts, and even, if you will, irreverence.' " She looked up. "What's irreverence?"

"You'll find out," said Paula.

" 'But Elliot Garfield and Mark Bodine's *Richard the Third* gives us less than a summer stock *Charley's Aunt*, without the good-natured and inoffensive humor,' " Lucy put down the paper. "Does that mean he didn't like it?"

A voice came from the next room. "The man has two months to live; he's a cynic."

Elliot appeared in the doorway. He still wore the

140

clothes he'd worn the previous evening, incredibly wrinkled and disheveled.

"Which one of you Scotch-taped my tongue to the roof of my mouth?"

"You want some coffee?" said Paula.

"Not unless you have some bicarbonate."

Paula smiled and poured him a cup. Elliot sat down heavily at the table and buried his face in his hands.

"No chanting today?" said Paula.

"Buddhist holiday," said Elliot. "Celebration of boilermakers."

"Congratulations," said Lucy.

Elliot looked at her. "For what?"

Lucy shrugged. "I didn't know what else to say."

Elliot reached over and pulled the *Times* away from her. "Why do you let your child read pornography?" he asked Paula.

The phone rang.

"You want Puffed Rice or Special K?" said Lucy.

"What are you having?" said Elliot as Paula picked up the receiver.

"Pizza," said Lucy.

"Pizza? For breakfast?"

"Sure. Scientists have found that pizza is very nourishing," said Lucy. "Almost a meal in itself. You get carbohydrate—is that right?—yeah, carbohydrate. And protein from the cheese. And vegetables from the tomato sauce. Cereal is junk compared to that."

"Very convincing," said Elliot.

"For you," said Paula. And then, into the phone. "Would you hold on just a moment, please? Mr. Garfield will be with you shortly."

"Very nice," said Elliot, crossing to the phone.

"Well done." Paula handed him the receiver. "Hello?"

"Elliot?"

"Yeh."

"Mark."

"Oh. Hello, Mark."

"Elliot, I've got some bad news. You sitting down?"

"Mark, it really doesn't matter. You can think of me as seated, if that would help."

"Elliot, Mrs. Morganweiss has decided to close the show."

"No!" said Elliot, feigning shock. "You mean after all the critical acclaim?" He wanted to open up to Mark, tell him how rotten a thing he'd done in wrecking Elliot's career, how juvenile and preposterous his ideas were. But Bodine spoke first.

"Listen, Elliot, I . . . uh . . . can't tell you how sorry I am about all of this. It's entirely my fault, I realize that, and I'll certainly make that clear to anyone who ever cares to inquire in the future. You gave me everything I asked for . . . and more. You were better than I, or anyone, had a right to expect, within the limits I confined you to. Listen, I . . . well, I've said it. I tried something, and it failed. Someday, perhaps, you'll be able to forgive me. Goodbye."

Elliot heard the click and put down the phone. You couldn't even yell at someone in this crummy world, he thought. Even that was taken away. The louse. What did Mark have to be nice for? Why was he so damn reasonable? He returned to the table.

"See?" he said. "There you go. The minute you think your world's collapsing, something wonderful happens."

142

"What?" said Lucy.

"They closed the show," said Elliot. "I don't have to do it any more. The American Theatre is saved."

Paula poured more coffee in his cup. "I am sorry."

Elliot shrugged. "Listen, everything works out. Now I'm free to take that other job."

"What other job?" said Lucy.

Elliot opened the *Times* and flipped through the pages, stopping at the Classified section. "I'm looking, I'm looking, I'm looking. Here." He read aloud. " 'You're in your thirties or forties and you feel life lies ahead of you. You've spent ten or more years in pharmaceuticals, preferably the marketing end, and you know the score. You're already earning 20 to 30 thousand, but your boss still doesn't recognize your real potential. You're a tough, shirtsleeves kind of guy, not afraid of hard work and extra hours, so long as the rewards are there. If you've read this far, and the description fits, drop us a line. We're a top-fifty East Coast drug company, and we have a truly exciting opening in suburban Baltimore. All benefits. Salary open. For the right man, this is the chance of a lifetime.' "

Elliot looked up. "Sounds perfect, no? I mean I'm a tough, shirtsleeves kind of guy."

Paula smiled. "Lucy, we're late. Go get your sweater."

Lucy crossed to the bedroom door. "Listen," she called back, "did you know that Spencer Tracy got terrible reviews the first time he was ever on Broadway?"

Elliot looked at her slyly. "No, he didn't."

"No?" said Lucy. "Oh. I thought he did." She disappeared into the bedroom.

143

Elliot turned to Paula. "You realize, of course, your daughter has a crush on me."

"I've noticed," said Paula.

"How do you feel about that, Mom?"

"Not to take away from your personal charm," said Paula, "but she had one on Tony, too."

"They're fickle at ten."

"And at six. She also had a big thing for her father."

Lucy came out of the bedroom, putting on her sweater.

"Wait for me downstairs," Paula said.

"Why?"

"Why? Because . . . I'm the mother, that's why."

"That's not an excellent reason."

"I'm not required to be excellent," said Paula. "Or reasonable. This is a dictatorship here."

"Cynthia said that's what they have in Venezuela. Only he calls himself a president."

"Downstairs," said Paula.

Lucy shrugged and left. Paula turned to Elliot. "So? What're your plans?"

"You mean my immediate plans? Oh. Well, first I'll have breakfast. Pizzas, maybe. Then I think I'll try an aborted suicide attempt. Maybe slash my wrists with an electric razor in the men's room of the Music Hall. After that, I'll think about welfare."

"But you're not going back to Chicago?"

"That hole? No. Siberia, maybe."

"I mean, your room is paid for. It belongs to you."

"Thank you," said Elliot. "That's very kind. It's nice to know you have something you can convert to ready cash. If I decide to leave, I'll give you an address and you can ship the room to me."

"If you stay," said Paula slowly, "I could use someone to help me out with Lucy."

144

Elliot raised his eyebrows.

"I start work today," said Paula, "and—"

"You never did tell me what kind of job."

"You never asked."

"Yeah. I guess I've been a little preoccupied. All right. I'm game. What kind of job?"

"Well," said Paula, "it's in the entertainment field, I guess you might say. I have to meet these men and be nice to them for a few hours and. . . ."

Elliot grinned.

"Auto show," said Paula. "I pose, along with the cars. You know, women and cars."

"I think the job you made up would be more appealing."

"Better paying, too, I'm sure. Anyway, the point is I won't be able to get back to make Lucy dinner. I guess what I'm saying—uh, asking—is. . . ."

"I accept," said Elliot.

"Good," said Paula quickly. She was surprised at her own genuine relief and happiness. "She has dinner around six usually. There are pork chops in the freezer. She'll probably ask for something crazy, but give her those. Have a nice day."

She turned and went out. Elliot looked after her.

"Cute," he said aloud. "Definitely cute."

Lucy and Paula walked to the bus stop on 77th Street and Broadway. Lucy held a typewritten sheet in her hand as Paula, eyes closed, recited.

"The SEEC-T is a lean-burn approach to engine combustion that allows the engine to use less gas and more air in the combustion mixture. A special intake . . . uh, a special intake . . . wait, don't tell me. . . ."

Lucy, who'd memorized the sheet ten minutes after looking at it, said, "Valve."

"I said. 'Don't tell me.' Why did you tell me?"

"You weren't going to get it."

Paula shot her an annoyed glance. "All right. A special intake *valve* introduces extra air into the cylinders. The effect is to package unburned . . . unburned . . . don't tell me. . . ." Her shoulders slumped as she gave up. "Tell me."

"Exhaust pollutants."

"*Damn!* Exhaust pollutants. How did you remember that?"

"It sounds like one of those breakfast cereals I never eat," said Lucy. "Exhaust pollutants."

"I think you need a five-year course in an Oriental garage to understand this stuff," said Paula.

They reached the bus stop and stood on line. "I was noticing you and Elliot look very good together," Lucy said.

"What?" said Paula loudly.

The Chinese man in front of them turned around. "She say, she notice you and Erriot rook vely good."

"Thank you," said Paula, embarrassed. She spoke to Lucy in a loud, angry whisper. "When? When did we look good together?"

A few other people in the line turned around, and Paula smiled at them.

"All the time," said Lucy.

"When, all the time?"

"Whenever you're together."

"We are *never* together."

"How could you never be together? He lives in the same house."

The Chinese man turned around, grinning. "You tell me, this bus go twenty-seven stleet?"

"I . . . I'm not sure," said Paula. "Tly . . . uh, try asking someone else."

He nodded and turned back, but did not address any of the other people.

"Besides," continued Paula to Lucy, "I'm a good inch and a quarter taller than he is."

"I never noticed. Maybe because I'm small, and always looking up."

"Maybe because you just didn't *want* to notice."

They sat near the rear of the bus, and Paula, eyes closed, mentally went over her lines again. "The SEEC-T engine," she muttered involuntarily, "with its advanced design, results in good performance plus better mileage."

A young, pimpled man in a black leather jacket leaned over from across the aisle. " 'Scuse me, what car you talking about?"

Paula opened her eyes. "What? Oh . . . The Subaru."

"The Subaru," repeated the man. "Oh, I thought you was promoting some American car."

"No, I—"

"Pieces of shit," the man said. "Don't get me wrong, I love this country, but our cars are shit. I bought one about a year ago, didn't run more'n a week before I had to fix it. Even the brakes didn't work. I finally sold it to my brother-in-law."

"Thank you for the advice," said Paula. She turned to Lucy. "And I must be at least two years older than he is."

"Who?" said Lucy. "Him?" She pointed across the aisle at the man in the black leather jacket.

"You know who."

"So what?" said Lucy. "Men prefer women of experience. I read it in *Cosmopolitan*."

"Lucy," said Paula, "how would you like it if

I took you and Seymour Stroock to a movie and dinner Saturday night?"

"*Seymour Stroock*? I *hate* Seymour Stroock! Don't do that!"

Paula smiled triumphantly. Chalk up another victory for the mature scheming mind over the immature scheming mind.

"Then lay off me and Elliot," she said with feigned sweetness. She looked past Lucy out the window. "Oh, here's your stop. Go. Get out of my life."

Lucy stood up, as did the Chinese man who'd been ahead of them in line.

"This isn't Twenty-seventh Street," Paula called out.

The man turned, and grinned. "Oh, understand," he said, as the bus stopped. "I no go there, only want to know if bus stop there."

He and Lucy got off.

"I'm getting to the truth, right?" Lucy called back to Paula's window. "The Shadow knows, heeheehee."

Paula shouted, "I hate you! I really really hate you!"

People turned to look at her as the bus pulled away.

"Well, I *do*," she said to the man across the aisle.

"I hate my brother-in-law," he said.

Paula closed her eyes and tried to see the words in her mind. . . . *with less emission than a standard engine and without any additional* . . .

The next word wouldn't appear, and she reached for the printed text. Gone! she realized suddenly. Lucy had taken it with her! She stuck her head out of the window and looked back. In the distance, a very tiny Lucy was climbing the front steps of her school, trying to remember something, anything at all, about the Canadian province of Nova Scotia.

Chapter 10

By the thousands, spectators thronged the 59th Street area before the Coliseum. Souvenir vendors were doing a booming business, as were the pretzel men, the chestnut men, and the local prostitutes. Paula, in blue blazer, white skirt, and red blouse stood with Donna on line at a hot dog stand.

"So?" said Donna. "How're you doing?"

"Eh, not bad. Considering I don't know what the hell I'm talking about."

Paula reached the head of the line. "Hot dog and Coke," she said to the vendor.

The man reached for a burned, grizzled-looking frankfurter.

"Uh, not that one," she said. "Can I have another?"

"Same thing, lady," said the vendor. "All beef. I only sell all beef. You want this one here?"

Paula nodded.

"You want it, you got it," continued the vendor, placing it on the roll and adding mustard and sauerkraut. "Any preference on which bottle of Coke?"

"Don't be wise," said Paula.

When Donna had gotten hers, they moved a few steps away.

"Listen," said Donna. "There're a couple of guys want to buy us some fettucine when we're through. The Cohen brothers. You've seen them? Over by the Ferrari exhibit."

"I didn't notice."

"Yeah. Sol and Moishe. Moishe calls himself Marvin. Very cute. Sol's the brunette."

"Cohen brothers? With Ferrari?" said Paula. The hot dog was unbelievably good.

"Are you kidding? They own about ten dealerships apiece. Anyway, you available?"

"Oh, thanks, Donna," said Paula. "Maybe some other night."

"We have only eight nights left. It's not as though you had something better waiting at home, right?"

"No, no." Paula guzzled down the last drop of Coke. "Maybe tomorrow, okay? Listen, I've gotta get back. Show time." She gave a little theatrical skip and waved goodbye.

Inside, she made her way through the crowds of people until she reached a gate where a uniformed man was taking tickets. She reached in a pocket and came up empty; she'd left her badge at the exhibit. Without pausing, she started through the gate.

"Hold it," said the man in uniform. "Ticket, please."

"Oh," said Paula. "Listen, I'm a model."

"Oh, yeah?" said the guard. "I'm a guard."

"No, no. A model in the show."

"How many miles a gallon you get?" said the guard, guffawing. And then, pleased with himself. "Hey, you got a nice set of headlights there."

151

"Look," said Paula, exasperated. "I'm late. I've gotta get back. Now open up."

The guard's face seemed to set.

"Please!" said Paula urgently.

He looked around. "I could lose my job if. . . ."

"You won't lose your job. I'm at the Subaru exhibit. I left my badge there. You can come with me, and I'll show it to you."

The man nodded and opened the gate. "Nice wheels, too," he called after her.

Paula fought through the bristling activity, almost overwhelmed by the lights, cameras, salesmen, book-sellers, and the centers of attention—the shiny, polished, sleek, ultra-plush symbols of sex, power, and status, the automobiles. ". . . zero to sixty in four minuscule seconds!" she heard some salesman lie as she passed.

At last she reached the Subaru exhibit and hopped lightly onto the giant, slowly rotating turntable. The other model handed her the mike and stepped off. Paula pretended to caress the hood of the little car with her hand, simultaneously adjusting the mike around her neck. She cleared her throat.

"The Subaru engine gets thirty-nine miles per gallon in highway driving and twenty-nine in the city, an extraordinary performance."

The small crowd watching the exhibit murmured and gestured.

"The SEEC-T is a lean-burn approach to engine combustion that allows the engine to use less gas and more air in the combustion mixture. A special . . . uh . . . intake valve introduces extra air into the cylinders—"

Near the rear of the immediate crowd, a man and a little girl were squeezing their way toward the front.

152

"The design," continued Paula, "eliminates the need for power and fuel-robbing—"

She spotted them then. Moving forward rapidly. Lucy and Elliot. I've got to be careful not to get flustered, she thought. She became flustered.

"—uh, eliminates the need for power and fuel-robbing, uh—"

Elliot winked at her.

"—things. The Subaru gives good performance plus better mileage with less emission than a . . . a standard engine, and . . . uh, without—"

In the audience, Elliot turned to Lucy. "She's up." He smiled broadly at Paula.

Paula tried desperately to look away. "—without any knocks, or noises, or that . . . that terrible banging sound. Uh, which, uh . . . as you know, can be terribly banging." Her head had completely emptied itself; her brain was in suspended animation.

She went on. "As you see—she banged on the side of the car—"the Subaru has two solid metal doors . . . one on each side . . . of the Subaru. This unique arrangement is, uh, well . . . for easy getting in and getting out . . . which must be done before and after driving . . . the Subaru."

Lucy looked at Elliot. "She's making it all up."

"The tires," continued Paula, the thin tones of panic just beginning to tinge her voice, "are very attractive, very, and are optional. . . ."

"That's quite an innovation," said Elliot to Lucy. "Optional tires. What's standard, water buckets?"

"The seats," said Paula, "front and rear . . . are made of, uh, rich, beautiful material. Material like you'd find in much better cars than . . . and they can easily be cleaned, of course, too. Very easily. Provided, of course, you first make them dirty."

In another part of the audience, Mr. Ishiburo,

assistant vice president of sales for Subaru, looked up from his conversation with Mr. Muraka, a salesman, who was also looking up. Both turned to listen to Paula more closely.

"The front windows are clearly visible, and designed for maximum . . . visibility . . . whether looking to the right, or the left, or even . . . you know, uh, straight. Straight ahead."

Elliot whispered. "Next to this my Richard looked like Laurence Olivier's. You know, seeing this is excellent therapy. They ought to use it for all disgraced actors."

"She's completely off the wall," agreed Lucy.

Paula was sweating profusely, but still maintained a fraudulent, semi-hysterical smile. "Likewise, the rear window is also designed for easy visibility. Plus —you can see out the back."

Mr. Muraka said, "Oi ding mushow ganza moo wush?"

"Must be making it up," answered Mr. Ishiburo.

"The steering wheel is not just a wheel. It's the most modern steering device ever devised. Deviced, I mean. Deviced? Anyway, the steering is easy and safe, and the brakes will stop you in any weather . . . uh, if you press on them, on the pedal. If you don't wish to stop, you merely keep your foot off the pedal! The Subaru is a truly remarkable economy car . . . and *Consumers' Guide* calls the Subaru a . . . uh, truly remarkable economy car."

She stood there for another moment, her mouth open as if to speak, but nothing came out. Finally, she said, "Thank you," unhooked the mike, and stepped quickly off the turntable.

Ishiburo was waiting. "Miss McFadden?"

"Oh," said Paula "Yes. Mr. Ishiburo, I—"

"Miss McFadden, you are perhaps in the creative writing business?"

"Well, no, I—"

"Advertising, then?"

"Mr. Ishiburo, I know the presentation. I just panicked for a moment and—"

"Perhaps, with all ah-respect, if you'd attended the ah-rehearsal—"

"My daughter was sick. I wanted to, but—"

"I thought you were sick. Your doctor—"

"Oh. Yes," said Paula quickly. "I was. See, I caught it from her."

"Ah," said Mr. Ishiburo. "Yes. So. It will not happen again though, now, will it?"

"Oh, no," said Paula, "I'm better now."

"I mean about forgetting." He stiffened, and began to quiver slightly. "Very ah-embarrassing, is it not?"

"Yes," whispered Paula. "Very."

"Good," said Ishiburo curtly, and he walked away.

Paula bowed and then went over to Lucy and Elliot.

"Thanks a lot!" she said. "I would have gotten fired, but he didn't know the English word for it. What are you doing here?"

Elliot arched his eyebrows. "You came to see me act, can't I see you?"

"This isn't—"

"Very nice. One constructive comment?"

"Really, you're—

"Study. Learn your lines. Then maybe next year you'll be ready for bigger parts. Like trucks. Or possibly tanks."

Paula turned to Lucy. "Did you have dinner yet?"

"No."

"No?" She looked back at Elliot. "It's after seven. What am I paying you for?"

"*Paying* me?" said Elliot. "One petrified pork chop and a stalk of aging brown celery does not constitute a payroll. Besides, I came to leave Lucy with you. I'm working tonight."

"He got a job," amplified Lucy.

"Didn't I just say that?" said Elliot.

"Acting?" asked Paula.

"I didn't say that," replied Elliot. He looked up into space and stroked his chin. "It's . . . uh . . . in the entertainment field, that's as much as I can tell you. I'll be home about two, so don't wait up."

Paula shook her head disgustedly.

"You look terrific," said Elliot. "I never knew you had a figure."

He patted Lucy on the head and walked away.

"He wears me out!" said Paula, staring after him. "That man wears me out."

Just before he reached the top of the escalator, Elliot saw the Subaru sales booth, and walked over.

"Howdy!" he said pleasantly, offering a hand to Ishiburo, who shook it vigorously, "J. T. Thomas, Houston, Texas."

"Ah. Yes. How you do?"

"Well, I'm doin' real fine," said Elliot. "Yes, sir, real fine! Fact is I'm in the taxi business back in Houston, an' I'll tell ya, that li'l girl back there"— he motioned toward Paula—"made a powerful impression with your Su-bay-ro."

"Ah, Yes. Subaru. Uh-huh. Yes."

"I'm in the market for a fleet, ya know, cover the downtown area. Your company handle something like that?"

"Freets? Oh, yes! Of course, we do many." Ishiburo was beaming from ear to ear.

"Tell ya what," said Elliot. "I'll be back the end of the week, and we'll sit down an' talk about it. If anythin' gets goin', maybe y'all can come down Houston way then, an' I'll show you my digs."

"Digs?"

"You know, surroundings. House, office, like that."

"Ah, yes. Digs." Ishiburo renewed his smile. "Yes, understand. You know, Mr. . . . ah . . . Thomas, I have feeling we speak before sometime, yes?"

"Doubt it," said Elliot. "Listen, pleasure jawin' with y'all, gotta run now. Tell ya, you oughta hang on real good to that girl."

He sauntered away. Ishiburo quickly looked at Paula, then at the departing Elliot. Gradually, a look of puzzlement displaced his smile.

It was on 8th Street near Sixth Avenue, a Village joint called the Golden Barn. The traffic past it consisted of every imaginable and unimaginable type of human being. College students with texts on partial differential equations, out-of-work Dixieland musicians, Iowa farmers in for a vacation, lesbians who lived in lofts on Great Jones Street, homosexual business executives soon-to-be-mugged after touring the gay bars, flocks of fifteen-year-old high school girls recently ignored at NYU fraternity houses, black cocaine pushers from Bed-Stuy, hardware salesmen from Flint, Michigan, junkie-prosties selling their diminishing flesh at five dollars per use.

A zoo parade of the species, thought Elliot. He himself stood right in front, out there in his threadbare, too-large purple coat with the gold buttons

157

(one missing), the epaulets, and the foolish matching hat. Elliot the doorman. Elliot the barker.

"Hey, come-one-come-all to the Golden Barn. See the exotic Lilah and the very sensuous Margene writhe and swirl together in a heated orgy of seething lust! See the girls' bodies touch and caress as they make—"

Someone tapped him on the shoulder, and Elliot looked around. Two seventeen- or eighteen-year-old boys were attempting to peek in the door.

"Hey," said the first boy, "Wha—what kind of, you know, show they got in there?"

Elliot opened the door a tiny crack. The crack offered a nearly subliminal glimpse of two women on stage, one black, one white, both topless and wearing the briefest of bottoms.

"Dirty!" whispered Elliot. "Very dirty! Filthy show! Next one starts in ten minutes."

The other boy was still staring at the door, even though Elliot had closed it. "Like what do they do?" he asked.

"They won't let me see it," said Elliot. "It's too dirty for the help." He opened the door again briefly. "You interested?"

Just then a heavy, masculine, red-haired woman emerged from inside. She wore a man's suit and spoke in a deep voice.

"Come on!" She snapped her fingers at Elliot. "Inside, quick!"

She was Mrs. Maloney, the manager, and Elliot assumed he was being fired. Must be for opening the door for the kids, he thought. Or something like that.

"What's wrong?" he asked.

"We got a drunk on stage," she said.

Elliot felt the fright shoot right through him. He had never had any training in dealing with drunks. He followed her in. On stage, two waiters were trying to restrain a huge man in an army jacket from getting at Lilah and Margene, who were cowering near a corner of the curtain. The army jacket is a bad sign, thought Elliot. The man might've been in the special forces, an ex-commando possibly, trained in dispensing instant death. Discharged from the service and unable to find work, he'd taken to drink and attacking sleazy exotics. The problem was that, even drunk, he still had seventy percent of his reflexes, could still kill the average man in eight seconds instead of the usual five when sober. *Doorman slain by Medal-Winning Green Beret.* The drunk swung a lazy punch at one of the waiters, catching him on the side of the cheek and sending him sprawling across the stage. Lilah screamed, and the customers applauded.

"Get that creep out of here," said Mrs. Maloney to Elliot.

"His jaw may be broken," said Elliot.

"I mean the drunk!" said Mrs. Maloney urgently.

"Who, *me*?" said Elliot. "I'm the doorman. When he comes out, I'll open the door."

"You want to get paid? Or not."

"All right, all right."

Elliot walked toward the stage. The patrons, a cross-section of the street traffic outside, seemed remarkably unperturbed.

"Here comes Superman to the rescue," a woman called out. "Looks more like Wonder Woman," said her companion.

The drunk landed a low right to the second waiter's abdomen, doubling him up and sending him rolling offstage.

Elliot approached cautiously. "Okay, take it easy now." He climbed the small steps to the stage. "Easy pal. I'm your friend . . . your buddy, okay?"

"Creep's gonna kill us," he heard Margene whisper loudly.

The drunk started for the girls.

"Hey," said Elliot, "why don't you sit down so we can go on with the show?" He raised his eyebrows and nodded.

"I just want a kiss," the drunk said thickly. "One little kiss, that's all."

"I hardly know you," said Elliot, unable to help himself. "I don't kiss on first dates."

The audience laughed, and there was scattered applause. Elliot raised his hands.

"Thank you, thank you." He turned back to the drunk. "They like us."

The man began weaving toward Elliot, his head cocked to one side. "Come here, you little twerp. I'll bust your stupid face in."

Suddenly, he didn't seem quite so drunk. Elliot backed away and circled. "No, no, they don't want to see that." He addressed the audience. "You don't want to see a little twerp get punched out, do you, folks?"

There was more applause. A few people whistled.

"Tough audience," said Elliot to the drunk. "Listen, pal"—he moved closer so that he would not have to speak as loudly—"can I talk to you a minute? Can we reason this out? Can we? What's your name?" He began to feel better. Perhaps no one had ever considered this man as a person.

"Earl," said the man.

"Earl what?" said Elliot.

It happened, or seemed to, in a kind of inevitable

slow motion. He *saw* the punch in plenty of time—a roundhouse, looping left—and raised his right hand to block the path to his ear. And that was the problem. His hand. Too late he realized it should've been a fist. The man's punch hit Elliot's fingers, deflected slightly, and caught him just under the eye.

"Earl *this*," said the drunk as the blow landed.

Elliot slid across the stage and off, landing at Mrs. Maloney's Thom McCan shoes. He stood up immediately, somehow, miraculously, having escaped being badly hurt. The audience was applauding and whistling.

"My first standing ovation," said Elliot.

He watched as Earl crossed the stage, grabbed the screaming Lilah by the arm, and bent his head in an attempt to kiss one of her nipples. Pressing her lips together, she kicked out at his left shin with a high-heeled, pointed shoe. Earl yelled, "Ahh!" and let go her arm. She followed up immediately, lashing out at the other shin. "Ahh!" Earl screamed, and hobbled away. He bent over to rub his legs. Margene, who'd circled around, came up behind him and kicked him viciously in the neck. Earl toppled and lay still. The audience applauded.

Three minutes later, two uniformed police arrived and hauled Earl off the stage.

"Another job well done," said Elliot, and started back for his post at the door.

"You're out," said Mrs. Maloney. "If you can't handle something simple like that, how're you going to take on the really rough guys?"

"You mean I'm fired?" said Elliot. The numbness was beginning to wear off his eye, and bright flashes of pain were erupting high in his cheek.

161

Mrs. Maloney peeled off a ten-dollar bill and handed it to him. "That's two hours at four dollars an hour, plus two dollars severance," she said.

Elliot took the ten. "That's most generous, most generous," he said. "I suppose the severance refers to my face, which nearly got removed from my head."

Mrs. Maloney had turned away.

"Can I at least have a piece of steak or something for my eye?" asked Elliot.

"Steak!" said Mrs. Maloney. "You want steak, yet! You know the price of chuck these days? Get outta here."

Elliot walked toward the door, weaving his way among the tables. A woman got up to dance, and as Elliot passed her place setting, he noticed a half-eaten piece of meat still on her plate. He grabbed it, held it to his eye, and ran out. I need it more than she does, he rationalized.

Paula worked the cold cream into her cheeks and chin and neck as Lucy spoke to her from the tub.

"You know what Cynthia Fein said?"

"Who's Cynthia Fein?"

Lucy shifted her position and adjusted her pajamas. The tub, of course, had no water in it. "The girl in my class with the braces and the big chest. Elliot picked me up at school today, and Cynthia saw him." Lucy took another bite of the banana she was eating.

"So?"

"Cynthia said he's got charisma."

"You don't even know what that means," said Paula.

"I do so," said Lucy. "I looked it up. And he does."

Paula put down the jar of cold cream. "All right, cut it out."

"Cut what out?" asked Lucy innocently.

"Stop trying to make something between us."

"*Me*? Cynthia Fein said—"

"Cynthia Fein my behind!" said Paula, turning angrily. "Stop pushing me."

Lucy sank down in the tub. "Who's pushing?"

"You are."

Lucy studied a tiny brown spot on her banana. "Your fingerprints are all over my back," continued Paula.

"Why? I never said—"

"He's okay, all right? Once in a while he even acts like a regular human being. But stop pushing me, because that man is not my type!" She stormed out of the bathroom.

Lucy, using the banana as a microphone, muttered a short commentary into it.

The door swung open, and Paula reentered. "I heard that. What did you say?"

"If you heard it, why are you asking?"

"*What did you say?*"

"I said," said Lucy, sinking down even farther into the tub "that your type never hangs around long enough to stay your type."

Paula stared at her, hurt and amazed. How could the child frame and express so accurately Paula's experiences with men? It was true, you should never underestimate children's perceptions. "That," she said slowly, "was a rotten thing to say."

"I know," said Lucy nonchalantly.

"Then why—"

"I just felt like saying it."

163

"Jesus!" said Paula. "Sometimes I can get"—she saw that Lucy was picking at a loose thread on her pajamas and seemed not to be listening—"so goddam furious with you!"

She reached suddenly into the tub and turned the "COLD" faucet sharply to the left. She walked out the door just as a cascade of icy water poured down on Lucy's legs.

"Hey!!!" Lucy jumped up, her pajama bottoms soaked. "What a stinky thing to do!"

Her face still embalmed with cold cream, Paula walked into the kitchen. She went to the cupboard and removed a box of animal crackers, then noticed that the door of the refrigerator was still open.

"Dammit!" she said aloud. "She leaves the refrigerator open! I'm gonna drown that kid."

She shut the door, and started back toward the bathroom. "Lucy," she yelled musically. "Oh, Lucy!" And then, lower. "Did mama's baby see *Psycho*, by any chance?"

As she passed Elliot's room, she noticed that the door was ajar. She peered in and saw legs stretched out on the bed. "Mr. Garfield?" she said tentatively. "Is that you?" Hesitantly, she entered the room.

"No," said Elliot. "Me is in perfect health. This isn't me." He lay flat on the bed, holding a piece of meat to his right eye.

"I didn't hear you come in," said Paula. "What happened to your eye?"

"I used it to stop a fist from going through my head."

"What . . . uh . . . kind of meat do you have on there?"

"Veal parmigiana. It was either that or potato salad." He shifted position slightly. "I'm out of work again."

164

He lifted the half-eaten meat off his eye and dabbed it around his cheek. Already, the area was turning bluish-purple. "I'm moving up, though," he said. "Last time I had one of these, I used a Big Mac for a bandage."

"Let me put some ice on that," said Paula.

Elliot followed her into the kitchen and stood in the doorway while she opened the refrigerator and removed an ice tray.

"You don't have to worry any more," he said.

She broke the ice out of the tray and spilled the cubes into the sink.

"I've decided to let you stay as long as you want," continued Elliot.

Paula grabbed a towel from the closet, scooped up the ice, wrapped it, and tied a knot so the cubes wouldn't fall out.

"It's my only hope for survival," said Elliot.

"Listen," said Paula, "something'll turn up." She handed him the icepack.

"You think so?"

"Lucy and Cynthia Fein think you have charisma," said Paula.

"And what do you think I've got?" said Elliot. He dangled the icepack loosely and began to swing it back and forth. "I mean, do I chariz you at all?"

"Put the pack on your eye."

"I'm not talking about my talent," said Elliot. "Talent-wise, I'm very secure. It's appeal-wise I'm a little shaky."

Paula cocked her head quizzically.

"The truth," said Elliot, rubbing his beard. "I can take it. Am I as adorable as I think I am?"

Paula looked at him and laughed. "You are outrageous. I can't keep up with your energy level. They must pick you up on CB radios in Alaska."

She walked to the doorway, sidestepping to avoid him. He sidestepped in the same direction, and she looked up.

"You get the feeling something's starting between us?" he said.

Paula shook her head. "I graduated from high school sixteen years ago—Thomas Jefferson—and that was the last time I heard that line."

She moved to the other side of the doorway, but Elliot moved even faster.

"Out of my way," said Paula. "Please. I have to sell my little Japanese cars in the morning."

"Is that why you have the Kabuki makeup on?" asked Elliot.

Paula ran a hand over her face. She gasped. The cold cream—she'd never taken it off! "Oh, God, and you let me stand there!"

She rushed to the sink, turned on the water, and began splashing and rubbing her face. There was no mirror handy, however, and so irregular blotchy patches still remained. Some water got into her eyes, and she closed them both tightly, and reached blindly upward with her left hand. "Towel! Can I have a paper towel, please?"

Elliot, who'd been standing passively in the doorway while she struggled, now walked over to the sink. He reached for the roll of towels, then stopped, turned to face her and kissed her softly on the lips.

Paula inhaled suddenly, then relaxed. The kiss, his lips, felt wonderful, pressing but not overly insistent, very slightly moist, full, *there*. She recovered a bit from the initial shock, parted her own lips a sixteenth of an inch, moved them in a very slow, circular motion. She felt his body against

166

hers, firm and muscular, tense, breathing. She felt herself begin to melt . . . and suddenly she backed away. Her eyes snapped open.

"Don't you ever do that again!"

"Your lips may say 'no, no,'" said Elliot, very pleased with himself, "but there's 'yes, yes' in your eyes. And, of course, vice-versa."

"Don't get cute with me," said Paula.

Elliot grinned. "You know your goddam nose drives me crazy?"

"My nose? What's wrong with my nose?"

"It's pug! Pug! It shoots straight down, then turns pug at the last minute." He leaned over quickly and jabbed a quick kiss at the side of her neck.

"Don't . . ."

"I think we got ourselves a hot infatuation here."

Paula pulled away. "Please. I have no time for romance."

"Make some. Leave work five minutes early. Skip going to the bathroom."

"I have a daughter—"

"I know."

"—who I'm trying to save from getting rickets."

Elliot moved a step closer and landed a pecking kiss on her still-wet left cheek. "I went bananas the first time I saw you through the crack in the door. I said, 'That's the best half a face I ever laid eyes on.'"

"Please don't make me laugh with my makeup on," said Paula, trying to hold back a smile. "I'll break my face."

Elliot pressed closer still. "I can smell your hair when you walk by my door."

"It's probably the hairspray."

"I could be sleeping, my nostrils wake me up and

say, 'Who dat comin' down de street?' I don't know why they talk with that accent, but they do."

"You're embarrassing me," said Paula.

"A little embarrassment is good for you. It's a very human emotion. Animals don't get embarrassed."

"I'm thirty-three," said Paula. "It's not supposed to happen to me any more."

Elliot looked at the ceiling. "If you were a Broadway musical, they'd come out humming your face."

She couldn't help it. She laughed, and as she did so, Elliot moved in and rained kisses all over her neck, her face, her ears, her mouth. Paula became flushed and weak. She was aroused.

"Oh, please," she said plaintively. "Don't do that. Don't make me feel happy. I hate that goddam 'it's wonderful to be alive' feeling."

Elliot kissed her on the forehead and held her shoulders.

"Don't come into my life," said Paula. "I just got through putting up all the fences."

"Can't I even see you to your door?" said Elliot. "It's a rough neighborhood." He wanted very much to hold her and keep showering her with kisses.

"Elliot—"

"Yes, call me Elliot. I've already bitten your neck."

Paula squirmed in his embrace. "Elliot . . . I'm praying. I pray to God this is all gone in the morning."

Elliot released her. "The hell you do! Listen, this isn't like some allergic rash, or something. I'll meet you in the kitchen tomorrow night."

Paula clicked her tongue.

"Tomorrow night," repeated Elliot. "And, uh . . . oh, don't dress."

Paula pushed past him and out of the kitchen. She ran quickly to her bedroom and closed the door behind her when she was inside.

Chapter 11

The telephone call came at nine-thirty in the morning, after chanting, after breakfast, after both Lucy and Paula had gone. They'd stared at each other a lot that morning, Elliot and Paula—long, heated looks, stares of lust. Funny, Elliot thought, the difference, the physical difference, an attitude can make in someone's appearance. She looked beautiful to him now. No qualifiers, simply soft and dreamy and loving. Long legs and a pug nose. And he must've looked the same way to her. Not long legs and pug nose, but also a certain softness, a certain physical aura of openness and warmth. They'd said little, and hadn't touched at all. Lucy had seemed kind of sullen. And then, when they left, there was the call.

"Hello?"

"Mr. Garfield?" A feminine voice.

"Yes."

"Mr. Garfield, my name is Maureen Keller and I got your number from Mark Bodine. I hope I haven't called at a bad time."

"These days I'd have trouble telling," said Elliot.

"The reason I'm calling, Mr. Garfield, is that I saw your *Richard the Third* the other day, and—"

"I think it just became a bad time," said Elliot.

"No, no, I spoke to Mark," said Maureen, "and he explained everything. But the reason I'm calling really is . . . uh, let's see, how do I put this? I—"

"If it's a death threat," said Elliot, "I could give you a standard form."

"On the contrary. I'm the agent for the Inventory, see, which is an improvisational group currently playing down on Charles Street, and we're currently looking to fill a position—"

Ellio felt his heart begin to pound in his chest.

"—and from what I saw in your performance, well, I wonder if you'd be available to come down and try out. I mean, would something like that appeal to you?"

Elliot thought: I've got to try not to babble. "Well," he said carefully, "it's certainly something I'd consider."

"Then you'll come down?"

"Yes. Sure. Why not?"

"Good. How's two in the afternoon?"

Elliot remembered he'd have to pick up Lucy at three. "Can we make it earlier, maybe?"

"How's one?"

"Fine."

"Good. Come to eight-eleven Charles Street. Just ask for me."

"Yes," said Elliot. "Okay. And . . . uh . . . thanks."

"See you."

There was a click, and the phone went dead. The Lord worketh his wonders in mysterious ways, thought Elliot. Not quite as tricky as John LeCarré, but very close.

The day dragged. Paula knew her speech now, and

171

it was a monotonous ramble. The crowds ebbed and surged, ebbed and surged, a moving, mindless tide, drawn by a shiny steering wheel here, an overhead door there, a model whose tight shorts revealed the cheeks of her ass, a hood with unusual louvers, a free brochure, a sample of upholstery, a look, a wink, a flashing light. There was no concentration any more. Now that Paula had her speech down pat, no one listened. Who cares about the Subaru? thought Paula after her lunchtime hot dog. She returned to the revolving stage, with its precious cargo. She suppressed an urge to kick the Subaru in the fender. At five o'clock, she felt like collapsing. By quitting time, she was just about to faint.

She emerged from a side door of the Coliseum and was immediately braced by the outside air. The lights on the marquee were already off. Behind her, a voice called, "Paula! Paula!"

She turned and saw Donna coming after her.

"Hey, where you running?" said Donna.

"I want to see Lucy before she goes to bed."

"Listen," said Donna, "I have a message for you."

"I'm listening."

"The Maserati people are throwing a small party upstairs at Twenty-One."

"How nice."

"Wait a minute. This guy Giorgio—the one who smells better than us?—he specifically asked for you."

"He asked for me?"

" 'I wanna see data beautifoola girla witha de laughing teetha.' "

"I can't," said Paula seriously.

"Why?"

"I have to get home."

172

"I don't understand," said Donna. "He's gorgeous. He told me to tell you he was."

Paula had already started walking. "Gee, if it was any other time. . . ."

The air had grown chill, and there was an excess of humidity that hinted of rain. Donna stood and watched Paula recede in the distance.

"What's a better time than when you're still alive?" she asked no one in particular.

Paula ran up the steps, got to her door, whipped out her keys—and stopped. She removed a small hairbrush from her pocketbook. Quickly, she smoothed down the sides of her hair, brushed back a few strands from her forehead. She put the brush away and opened the door.

Something was hanging. Paula approached more closely. In the entranceway, a piece of cardboard dangled from a string taped to the ceiling. The cardboard had writing: *See note pinned on sleeping child.* Paula walked into her bedroom and saw Lucy stretched out, asleep. Pinned to her nightgown was a piece of paper. For an instant, Paula remembered Tony, his letter under the knob of the TV. She read the note on Lucy.

This is Sleeping Child. Kiss her good night and come up to roof for private party. Dress—formal. Paula smiled, leaned down, and gave Lucy a kiss. Outside the apartment she climbed the steps rapidly.

She leaned hard on the heavy door to the roof, and it finally opened to the inky nighttime blackness. She stepped out gingerly seeing nothing.

"Elliot? Elliot, are you here? Say something, I don't like this."

Suddenly she heard soft music, a guitar. And then the rasp of a match being struck, the sudden glow of a candle. Paula crossed the rooftop, heading for the light. She made out a wooden box, set upright, and two of her own kitchen chairs placed beside it. As she came closer, she saw two glasses on the box, and a bottle that could only be champagne. A voice that was almost Humphrey Bogart's said from somewhere behind her, "I told you it was formal, kid."

Paula spun around, practically landing directly on Elliot, who'd sneaked up right behind her. He was wearing a 1930's-type tuxedo. She felt like laughing and crying simultaneously.

"The party has to be over by nine a.m.," said Elliot. "Otherwise it's another five bucks for the suit."

And then he folded his arms around her, and they began to dance, spinning and twirling over the rooftop in time to imaginary music.

"Don't panic," he said. "Even Ginger was nervous the first time she danced with me."

He began humming "Dancing Cheek to Cheek" in her ear, and Paula felt the tears slip out of her eyes and down the side of her nose.

"What are you crying about?" said Elliot.

Paula shrugged. "Kill me, I'm a sucker for romance."

"Elliot Garfield," said Elliot, "is a many-faceted individual."

He held her tightly and closed his eyes. He whispered in her ear. "I got a job."

"Seriously?"

"Yes. A real job. A real *acting* job."

"You're kidding."

"Nope."

"You did?"

"Yup."

"Where?"

"The Inventory. An improvisational group on Charles Street."

"Well, that's wonderful. Fantastic."

"They saw *Richard the Third* and said if I could do that, I could do anything."

Suddenly, a huge, jagged, luminous spike of lightning seemed to irradiate the entire sky. An instant later, a dull rumble of thunder rolled in from the distance.

"Oh, no," said Paula, frightened for a moment. "Don't let it rain."

"Oh, I think I will just this once," said Elliot.

Paula shook her head.

"Don't worry about it," said Elliot. "The suit is too big for me, anyway."

"When did you audition?" asked Paula.

"This afternoon. Improvisation, you understand. With this girl, Linda. Very talented."

"Is she pretty?"

"No, no. Ugly. Very unpugged nose."

"Good," said Paula.

"I did Abraham Lincoln. Mary Todd is out of town, and General Grant takes me to a cat house in Virginia. I'm trying to be very dignified, you know. 'Now, now, young lady, don't pull the beard. I'm the Pres—' "

Paula pulled his head close to her face and kissed him long and deeply on the lips. There was another streak of lightning, another clap of thunder, and then it began to rain. Heavily.

"Big drops," said Elliot. "My father used to say big drops meant the rain won't last."

"Don't stop," said Paula, her arms still around his neck. "I never danced in the rain."

"The hell with the dancing," said Elliot. "My pizza's getting drenched."

They let go of each other, scooped up the champagne and pizza and chairs, and ran to the door of the building. Paula tugged, but it failed to open.

"Let me," said Elliot, moving in front of her. The rain kept pouring down. He pulled hard, but nothing happened. He bent low and spoke to the doorknob. "Fucking door, open, or I'll kill ya. Open, you son-of-a-bitch-bastard-fucking door." He yanked and turned, and the door gave. He and Paula scrambled inside. "Just takes a little technique," he said, when they were safely out of the rain.

He re-lit the candle and set it on the stairs. They began to eat and drink.

"You get the feeling we're eating wet tennis sneakers?" said Elliot. He bit into another slice. Paula sipped the champagne.

"So what happened when you found out about this other girl and Tony?" said Elliot.

"Bobby," corrected Paula. "Tony comes after Bobby." She shrugged. "Well, it happens all the time on the road. He's gone six months with a play, and he gets lonely. The only time you have a good marriage is when your husband is in a flop. He's broke, but he's home."

"Where'd you meet Tony?"

"I'm ashamed to tell you."

"Why? Was it in some filthy perverted place like a museum?"

"I saw him in *The Iceman Cometh* at Circle-in-the-Square."

"And that wasn't all who cometh, was it?" said Elliot, teasing.

"He wasn't very good . . . but he was gorgeous."
Elliot rolled his eyes toward the ceiling.

"Couldn't stop looking at him," said Paula.
"Don't laugh. I waited till he came out of the stage
door and introduced myself."

"Happens all the time," said Elliot. "To other
actors."

"Like a regular groupie," continued Paula. "A
week later I moved in with him. I used to do things
like that."

Elliot crunched down on a last bit of crust.
"Why?"

Paula snickered. "You ever dance in the chorus
of a musical?"

"Not that I remember."

"Well, the boys usually have higher voices than
the girls. Ten years of that, and you get very hung
up on macho men."

Unconsciously, Elliot thrust out his chest.

"Thank God I've gotten through *that* period,"
said Paula.

"I'll let the preceding remark pass," said Elliot.
He looked up and caught her eye.

"Are we going to sleep with each other tonight?"
asked Paula.

Elliot leaned back and grinned. "I doubt if sleep
will enter the picture," he said.

She was staring at him.

"I'll tell ya," said Elliot, "of all the right-up-
front girls I ever met, you're right up front." He
narrowed his eyes. "How do you feel about it?"

"Nervous," said Paula. She nodded. "A pushover,
but nervous."

They both began to giggle.

They entered Elliot's room on tiptoes, and as

soon as he had the door closed he began to kiss her all over. She felt the heat begin to rise in her body, the sensitive swelling sweep over her breasts, the aching sweetness fill her loins. He blew lightly in her ears and flicked his tongue in and out. After a few moments he began to undress her, unbuttoning her blouse and skirt, unhooking her bra, leaving her in panties and high-heeled shoes.

"Nice," he said, backing away to look. "Very, very nice. We might be able to give you a centerfold, Miss McFadden."

He sat on the bed and began to strip. After removal of each garment, he took Paula's hand in his own and kissed each finger. The sensation went through her like electricity, finding its way to her groin. By the time he was naked, she was panting. He brought her close and kissed her; their tongues met and caressed in Paula's mouth. Finally, mercifully, as she began to moan, he slipped his hand between her legs.

It was a fantastic night. As she had guessed—hoped—Elliot was a beautiful, sensitive lover. A skilled, knowledgeable lover and, best of all, a concerned lover.

"My enjoyment is inseparable from yours," he'd said after their second time.

"I enjoyed like crazy," said Paula.

"I thought I detected that," he said. "Although some people will whimper at the drop of a hat."

She left his room about five-thirty in the morning and made her way to her own bedroom. Soundlessly, by the first dim shafts of morning light, she tiptoed to the bed and slipped under the covers.

Lucy stirred and sat up. "Where were you?"

"Oh. You're up? I couldn't sleep, so I went inside to read."

178

"What did you read?"

Paula looked at her steadily. *"The Life of Lincoln.* What's the difference? Go back to sleep."

She sank down, and Lucy lay back beside her. Nearly a minute had passed, and Paula was almost asleep, when Lucy said, "When do I move back to my old room?"

The bacon was beginning to curl up, and the aroma of its cooking filled the kitchen. Paula shut off the flame and dumped the contents of the pan onto a paper towel, which the grease soaked through immediately. After a moment, she put the bacon strips onto a plate and carried the plate over to the table. She sat down next to Lucy, who stared moodily at a dish of sardines.

"Want some?"

Lucy shook her head once, but did not look up.

Paula was picking desultorily at the bacon when Elliot appeared in the doorway. He gave a little theatrical skip.

"Good morning, everybody! Please, no applause."

He came over to the table and sat down. "And now for a little defilement of the old temple," he said, and began to nibble on a piece of bacon. "Goodies like this can make the temple collapse."

He looked from Paula to Lucy, but neither acknowledged him.

"And what's new this morning?"

No answer.

"A little silent spring, eh?" said Elliot, his jauntiness undiminished.

Paula caught his eye, then shifted her gaze to Lucy, and finally back to him. She gave a little shake of the head.

"There is *nothing* new this morning," said Elliot.

"Okay." He bit into a second piece of bacon. "I don't like it so crisp," he said. "And I don't like it meaty. Soft and fat, that's for me."

Lucy had not raised her head.

"They say this kid Lindbergh is gonna try to fly the Atlantic."

No response.

"James Stewart's gonna try it in the movie."

No response.

Paula said, "She didn't sleep too well last night."

Lucy's head snapped up. "I guess no one did." She rose from the table and picked up her books from the floor. "See you tonight."

She left the room and a moment later Elliot heard the outer door open and close.

"We've been found out, have we?" he said. "Funny, I thought the kid was rooting for us."

"Don't call her 'kid,'" said Paula. "She doesn't like to be called 'kid.'"

"Ohh? Sorry. In Chicago it's an expression of endearment. Like, 'Hi ya, kid,' or 'How's it goin', kid.'" He reached out and put his hand under Paula's chin. "What's wrong, kid?"

"Nothing."

"Glad to hear it. Any buttered toast—as long as I'm killing off my body."

"She's scared," said Paula, "that's all."

"Lucy?"

"She's afraid what happened before is going to happen again."

"What are you two, partners? I thought it was just you and me last night."

"What happens to my life affects hers," said Paula.

"I'll accept that," said Elliot.

"And I'm scared, too."

"But you don't have to be. I really am a wonderful, sensitive, nice person. I can get references from three clergymen and an orthodontist."

"Listen," said Paula, a pleading look in her eyes, "would you be terribly hurt if we just forgot about last night?"

"It's too late," said Elliot. "I've already made the entry in my diary."

She stood up from the table, cleared the empty dishes, and began washing them in the sink. "Look at me."

"I am. Very nice. Top-rated tush."

"I'm standing here with sweaty palms, and I have my hands in cold water. I don't even know what you're thinking this morning, what's on your mind."

"I'm thinking of bacon grease," Elliot said.

"Instead of asking me so many goddam questions—"

"What questions? Oops, there's one."

"—you can at least say to me, 'Last night was wonderful.' "

"Last night was wonderful."

"Instead of worrying about your lousy breakfast and your buttered toast, you can look at me and say, 'I'm crazy about you.' "

"I'm crazy about you."

Paula turned around. "Oh, it's easy enough to say after I've told you to say it."

"I was going to say it myself, but I didn't get the chance."

"Why couldn't you touch me?" continued Paula. "And I don't mean in a filthy way, either. I mean hold my hand, stroke my hair, let me know that there was some really nice feeling that existed between the two of us."

Elliot stood up. "There was. I mean *is*. There

really is." He walked toward her, but she backed away.

"Forget it. It's too late. Not if I have to think of everything for you." Paula pounded on the edge of the sink with her fist. "Oh, my God, I must be crazy! Crazy! I keep doing the same damn thing to myself over and over again."

"Paula—"

"When am I ever going to learn?"

"There's nothing to learn. This isn't like algebra. Each situation is different."

"Listen," said Paula, "I'm really not up to falling in love again. It's too much work."

"Do it lying down."

"I think," said Paula, "we would all be a lot better off if you packed up your things and left. Nothing personal."

Elliot glared at her. "*Now* I know why they all left." He pointed with his index finger. "Crackers! Animal crackers, lady! You have a severe case of emotional retardation."

He started for the door of his bedroom. "I am not leaving, I am *escaping*."

"You don't—"

"If any mail comes for me, keep it! I am not giving any forwarding addresses!"

He entered his bedroom and slammed the door hard behind him. Paula felt a knotted constriction in her throat, felt her eyes begin to water. A moment later the door opened, and Elliot stood there holding his empty suitcase.

"But, in passing, I would just like to say that last night was terrific."

"Elliot—"

"The Super Bowl of romance. I give it a fat nine on a scale of ten. You get one off for burping your wine, but all in all a very respectable score."

"Don't you get glib about last night!" said Paula angrily.

"Glib is not the same as articulate," said Elliot.

"It was *important* to me," said Paula.

Elliot was exasperated. "Could you lower your neurosis a minute, please? I'm not finished."

"I think you are."

"Don't ever tell me when to get affectionate. I touch when I want to touch. I fondle when I want to fondle."

"Oh?"

"Yeah. Oh. I was planning to touch you all during my eggs and fondle you right through my coffee." He jabbed a finger straight up. "However, there is no touching during my toast. Toast, I have alone."

Paula almost smiled, but caught herself at the last second.

"You want to know what your problem is?" said Elliot.

"No, but you're going to tell me."

"You love to love somebody, but the minute they take the initiative like I did last night, it scares the pants off you—nothing off-color intended."

"That's ridiculous."

"You didn't wait outside any stage door for me; I approached first. Right?"

She didn't answer.

"I *touched* first," Elliot went on. "And you can't handle that, can you?"

"That," said Paula, "is laughable. And silly. You're a silly man. You're the silliest man I ever met."

"You *know* I'm right," said Elliot.

"I know nothing of the kind."

"And you know yourself too well to ignore what I'm saying. You know what we got here?"

"A mess."

"*Taming of the Shrew* is what we got here. Despite the fact, Kate, that you are a large pain in the arse, last night was the best thing that ever happened to me, girl-wise, and if you weren't behaving like such a horse's rectum this morning, we could have been touching and fondling right up till five o'clock when I have to go to rehearsal."

Paula thought back to the night, to its glorious sensual delights.

Elliot stepped back into his room. "Personally, madam, I think you blew it." He closed the door.

Paula stood there, thinking. She had always leveled with herself, and she did so now. The man had spoken the truth. *Know ye the truth, and the truth shall make ye unhappy.* But it didn't have to. All she had to do was open her mouth very, very wide and swallow an extremely large chunk of pride. And a big reward waited. She breathed deeply, then crossed to Elliot's door, hesitated, and finally opened it.

"Don't put the suitcase on the bed," she said, entering the room.

Chapter 12

By two-thirty, Lucy had written "I must not talk in class" four hundred and thirty times. Mrs. Fanning, of course, had not forgotten the assignment, and had told her, "If you can't seem to do it for homework, perhaps you'll have greater success right here." And so Lucy had skipped the work on the day's dittos to concentrate on "I must not talk in class."

"How'd you ever get it all done?" she whispered to Cynthia.

"My brother helped me," said Cynthia. "He's seven, and he said it was fun for him. Also my mother."

"Your mother?"

"Oh, yeah," said Cynthia. "She's very concerned with my schoolwork and stuff. She goes—"

"Girl!" came Mrs. Fanning's voice from the front. "I see you, girl. And your friend, too. Be quiet now."

Lucy and Cynthia resumed their work. Cynthia traced from a map the path of the Orinoco River. Lucy wrote the word "must" twenty-five times, one under the other. After about ten minutes, Cynthia leaned over cautiously.

"How's you-know?"

Lucy shrugged. "Beats me."

"Do he and your mom get all—"

"I don't know what they do, and I don't care."

"Hey," said Cynthia. "What's the matter? I thought he was real dynamite."

"I really don't feel like—"

"All right!" yelled Mrs. Fanning. "That's it. Each of you gets another three hundred times 'I must not talk in class.' And it's due tomorrow."

"I'll just add it on to what I'm doing," said Lucy resignedly.

At five after three the two girls walked down the steps of the school and out onto the street. It was a sunny day, somewhat windy, and Lucy's hair blew in the breeze. Behind her, she heard hoofbeats. And then a familiar voice called "Lady Anne!" When she looked around, a hansom cab had pulled up to the curb beside her, a brown and white horse in the lead, a driver up front, and Elliot leaning out.

"The Black Prince is dead," he said, affecting a British accent. "England is yours."

She looked at him without smiling, and he dropped the accent.

"Don't you want England? Spain, maybe? Spain I can get you cheap."

"What are you doing in that thing?" said Lucy.

"Get in, quick. The horse has a meter on him."

Cynthia, who'd stopped along with Lucy, giggled.

"Where to?" asked Lucy.

"We are going home," said Elliot dreamily. "To Tara." He hummed the theme from *Gone with the Wind*. "Will you get in?"

He opened the door, and Lucy stepped up into the cab. Elliot smiled at Cynthia.

"Cynthia Fein, right?"

She nodded and smiled back.

"Listen," said Elliot. "I think you have charisma, too."

Cynthia put her hands on her hips and addressed Lucy. "Did you tell him?"

Lucy shrugged.

"Well, I never said that," yelled Cynthia as the cab began to pull away. "Wait'll I get you, Lucy!"

They drove around for about twenty minutes, then went in for a hot dog, and finally climbed a long flight of steps that led to the cable car that went to Roosevelt Island.

"I would've liked to ride more in that carriage," said Lucy when they were on the car.

"Me, too," said Elliot. "Unfortunately, the driver wouldn't take Confederate money."

The panorama of New York spread out before them—the barges on the East River, the tugs, the twin towers, the bridges, smokestacks, people. Still full of life, thought Elliot. Like a dying man who doesn't know he's had it. On a day when the arthritis doesn't hurt, and he can breathe, and his knees don't buckle, he thinks he can live forever.

"You wanna go to my opening tonight?" he said to Lucy. "I owe you a good time after the last one."

Lucy looked out and down. "I have homework."

"What are you sore about?"

"Nothing."

"Is the nothing me and your mom?"

"It's none of my business."

Elliot wagged his head. "Well, since you and I will be exchanging rooms tonight, I think it *is*. Only I'm a little old-fashioned. I want your approval."

"Me?" said Lucy with mock ingenuousness. "I'm only ten years old. I'm not allowed to vote yet."

Imagine, thought Elliot. Her age, and already she knows how to use sarcasm. Must be inherited from her mother. A gene for sharp-tonguedness. "I like your style, kid, I really do."

Lucy shot him a scathing look.

"Oops, sorry," said Elliot. "I forgot. You don't like being called 'kid.'"

Lucy slumped down in her seat. "I'm a kid, it fits."

What is going through her head? wondered Elliot. On what level do I communicate with her? She's a child, yes, but a child who's seen a lot, been knocked around a lot. Did this make her equivalent to an adult? Could you talk to her like an adult?

"Do you like me?" he blurted.

"You're wasting a lot of money," said Lucy morosely. "I'm not enjoying this ride."

"Answer my question," said Elliot loudly, and an old man sitting in front of them turned around briefly. "Do you like me?"

"Ask Cynthia Fein," said Lucy.

"Lucy—"

"She's crazy about you. Of course, she doesn't know you, which may or may not help."

"I'm going to keep asking till I get an answer," Elliot said.

"Is this an interrogation? Is this what the Germans used to do?"

"Do you like me?"

Lucy looked at the ceiling. "Is there any place you can throw up on these things? I think I'm getting nauseated."

"Lucy . . ." said Elliot determinedly.

She looked around. "Better yet, I think I'll just get out."

"Answer me, goddammit!" Elliot felt like shaking

188

her. "Yes or no. It makes no difference to me either way, because I'm moving in with your old lady, anyway, but I want to hear it first from your own lips. Yes or no!"

Lucy began to sob.

You're putting too much pressure on her, thought Elliot. *There* was your answer. She might have the mouth of an adult, but she hadn't the mind. The protective shield of experience. He put a hand on her shoulder.

"No!" she said.

"What?"

"Yes."

"Was that yes?" Elliot asked.

"No. I mean yes. It was yes."

"A lot?"

"Yes." She began to bawl then, really crying, the tears exploding from her eyes.

"A really, really, REALLY lot?" pressed Elliot.

"Yes."

"What?"

"Yes!"

"Can't hear."

"Yes, yes, YES, YES!"

The man in front swiveled to give another look. He'll probably turn me in to the cops at the end of the ride, thought Elliot. Child molester.

"Well," he said, "as much as you like me, it's not one one-thousandth as much as I'm nuts about you. Swear to God, Luce."

He hugged her close then, and in that moment, with the city passing under them, he knew that the word was not "like" or "nuts" or "crazy about." He loved her, pure and simple. Loved. He felt for her as deeply as he could feel about anything. Their faces touched, and her tears ran down his cheeks, and soon they were mingled with, and indistinguishable from, his own. He said, "I am certifiably nuts about you *and* your ditsy mommy. Now blow *that* into your handkerchief."

"I don't have a handkerchief."

Elliot pulled a tissue from his pocket, but it tore while he was getting it out. "No good," he said. "I guess you'll just have to cry on the people."

On the way home, near their house, Lucy pointed out the puddle-that-never-dried, the one that had baffled her for ages. "It's very mysterious," she said. "You can see all colors in it. Like a rainbow."

"Oh, sure," said Elliot. "There's a thin layer of oil on top of the puddle. The colors appear because changing thicknesses of oil cause reflections at different light frequencies to cancel or add. The film probably also reduces evaporation."

"Holy . . . you're unbelievable!" exclaimed Lucy.

"I was always excellent in physics," said Elliot nonchalantly. "Which, naturally, is why I became an actor."

They rode down the center escalator of the Coliseum, and Donna thought she was hallucinating.

"I thought for a minute I heard something," she said, "but I know I didn't really hear it."

"You heard it," said Paula.

"Say it again."

"You heard it."

"I didn't hear it."

"Elliot is moving in with me."

"Oh, my God," said Donna. "*Moving in with you?* You jest, good friar. Surely, you jest. You mean *the two of you together?*"

The escalator reached bottom. Paula looked

around to see if anyone was listening. "A little louder, Donna. They didn't hear it in the street."

"Oh, God!"

"Please! Will you, please?"

"What?"

"Don't say, 'Oh, God.' Because I've been saying it all day. I'm shaky enough. Be encouraging. I'll *pay* you to be encouraging."

Donna shook her head. "When are you gonna learn?"

"I've learned. I went to school twice, and flunked."

"But he's different, right?"

"He *is* different. This is a good man, Donna. He's sweet and he's gentle and he's funny and he's loving."

"And he's an actor."

"Only by trade. By birth he's a person."

The theater held perhaps a hundred people. Even raucous applause from a hundred people doesn't sound like much. Elliot and Linda came on stage in pitch blackness, set up their stools, and sat down.

"Can we have the house lights up, please?" called Elliot loudly.

The lights came on, and he could see Lucy, sitting right in the first row.

"Okay," said Elliot to the audience, "now it's your turn. A little improvisation now. How many authors have we got out there tonight, eh?"

There was some scattered clapping.

Twenty-three authors, thought Elliot. Not a bad night. "Okay, give us the situation and the characters. Linda and I will do the rest. All right?"

No answer.

"All right. Who's got a situation? Come on, I see a hand." Thank God, he thought.

A girl spoke out. "A boy calling a girl for a date."

"A boy calling a girl for a date," repeated Elliot. "All right. Who's the boy?"

"Albert Einstein," said another girl.

"All right, we have Albert Einstein for the boy. And the girl is . . ."

"Gertrude Stein," yelled the first girl.

The audience laughed and applauded.

"It's possible," said Elliot. "Their mothers could've arranged it. Okay, Albert Einstein calling Gertrude Stein for a date. . . ."

He leaned over to Linda. She was a full-figured girl bordering on fat, and some places she crossed the border. Her face was a sort of Elaine May-Louise Lasser combination, but she had a bigger nose than either. She was schizoid, paranoid, manic-depressive, pleasant, delightful, and very talented. "I'll start," whispered Elliot. "Any problems?"

"My ass itches," said Linda.

"I told you to put paper on the seat," whispered Elliot. "All right, here we go."

He pantomimed dialing the phone as the house lights dimmed.

"Fife . . . seven . . . nein . . . tzvei . . . fuften tzvantek . . . square root of three . . . und six to the eighth power of a parallelogram."

He waited for the imaginary ringing. "Ring, ring, ring . . . und final ring."

Linda pantomimed picking up the phone. "Hello is hello is hello?"

"Allo? Miss Shtein?"

"Yes. This is Miss Stein. Who is calling is calling is calling?"

"Vot? Could you shpeak up, pleez?"

"I'm sorry, I was eating my brownie."

"A brownie. How do you get a camera in your mouth?"

"I'm sorry," said Linda, "but I'm very busy living my autobiography. Who is this?"

"This is Albert Einstein. Relatively long distance from Princeton."

"Oh, Princeton. How are things over there?"

"Not bad. Ve beat Dartmouth today, twenty-one to seven pi square."

"Isn't that nice?" said Linda. "One moment, please. Pablo, will you stop crying? I'm sick of your blue period. Hello? Yes, I'm sorry. You were saying—"

"You sound busy. I'm not disturbing you, am I?"

"No, no. Not at all. I was just taking a bath— Alice, stop splashing, I'm on the phone. Go on, Albert."

"Vell, you don't remember me, but ven ve vere eight point three seven years old, if you'll forgif ze approximation, I sat next to you in math—"

"Math?"

"I think it's short for mathematics, although who knows from these things. Anvay, I sat next to you."

"Were you the one with the wild, frizzy, flyaway hair and the faraway look?"

"No. I vas ze vun viss ze straight black hair, und ze plastered-down-vith-vasoline look. Und you said, *"Vash* it, for crise sake, *vash* it!"

"One moment, Albert. Ernest Hemingway just walked in. What are you looking for, Ernie? A moveable feast? It's right over there. Rolling." She lowered her voice to a stage whisper. "He wants a moveable feast, let him chase a Bungalow Bar truck." Back to full volume. "You see it, Ernie? It's across the river and into the trees. I'm sorry. You were saying, Albert—"

"No. I vasn't saying Albert. I vas saying zat I vashed my hair, und I grew up, und I'm doing very vell, sank you. I von three Nobel prizes und ze *Jumble* contest in ze *Daily News,* und I'm making sixty-five dollars a month teaching school."

"Oh, Jesus!"

"Iss somesing wrong?"

"Scotty Fitzgerald just threw up on Zelda. Pablo's cleaning it up with a brush. Oh, Pablo, it's a masterpiece! I'll buy it. Go on, Alsy!"

"Alsy?" said Elliot. He tried to gauge the mood of the audience. The laughs had been pretty consistent near the beginning; now he sensed some restlessness. It was time to begin winding this one down.

"Vell, I was thinking about you yesterday," he said. "I vas out on der lake, nuclear fishing. Und I said to myself, 'Albert, you are not getting any younger. Time is passing.' This is the vay I sometimes talk. Anvay, den I actually saw time passing."

"What did it look like?" Linda asked.

"It looked . . . vell . . . it looked exactly the same as ven time iss coming *at* you. Only now you see it from the back, passing. I drew a diagram of it. I'll send it to you. You can frame it. Und I decided to call you up and ask you to go to the Physicists' Ball, sometimes referred to as the Physicists' Spheroid. It's a dance for those in ze profession. Very goot band zis year, supposedly, Robert Oppenheimer and his Protons. Good food, hydrogen and tonics—you vill love it."

"When is it?"

"Saturday night . . . from ten o'clock—to infinity."

He stood up then, and Linda followed.

Paula lay cuddled in Elliot's arms. It was night-time, and they were naked and in bed.

"You know what I would like more than anything in the whole world?" said Paula.

"I can't again right now," said Elliot. "Give me about twenty minutes."

"I mean next to that. You know what it is? My very own living room set. The women libbers will kill me, but God, how I love being a housewife."

Elliot's mind had drifted off. "What a nice feeling," he said. "To hear real applause. I took the entire audience's names and addresses. We'll have them over to dinner one night."

"And we definitely have to repaint this bedroom, okay?"

"What?"

"I'm redecorating," said Paula. "What color do you want the bedroom?"

"Jewish," said Elliot.

A few days later, Paula's job at the Auto Show ended, and the redecorating began in earnest. A bulky man with a thin mustache came and covered everything with heavy spotted canvas. He set down a tray and some cans, and began to mix up some plaster.

"Are you the only one?" said Paula. "Don't you have an assistant?"

"Just me," said the man. "Arnie-the-ox. I used to have a guy helped me sometime. Little guy. Little guy with a beard. Never liked him."

"Why didn't you like him?"

"I don't know, really," said the painter. "I think because he was little. I never liked little guys. So one day I got rid of him. 'Find yourself another job, Sherman,' I told him. That was another thing."

"What?"

"I never liked the name Sherman."

Later in the day, after Paula had offered him coffee, which he refused, he began to open up on his trade.

"See, yer amateur, he only wants to get to the fun part, the slopping-on part, you know, the actual painting. The guy in the business knows the secret is in your preparation. You seen how much time I spent on the spackling?"

"Well, yes, I noticed you were very careful."

"That's right, because that's where it pays off. And you take your paint. Some'll tell ya your pigment is everything. You get the color, they say, you got the job licked. You know what I say?"

Paula shook her head.

"I say bushwah!" yelled Arnie. He pounded the floor. "Base! There's your foundation. You get a good base, a quality base, and you'll have a quality job. Forget pigment! The secret is in the base."

"You sound very knowledgeable," said Paula.

Three hours later, she and Arnie stood by a nearly-completed wall, comparing it to the color of a light-blue shirt.

"I told you like this shirt," said Paula. "What you have is nearly purple."

"I guess I should've spent more time on the pigment," said Arnie glumly.

He re-did the wall, and came back the next day to finish the room. An hour after he left, the moving men arrived with the new couch.

"Kanicki brothers, ma'am," said a very short, squat, powerful fellow at the door. Paula could see a thin, much younger, blond boy standing behind him. "We got your couch on the landing below, Miss, so if you could tell us where you want it, we'll bring it right up."

"Sure," said Paula, pointing out a location.

She watched as the squat man went down to the landing, while the blond boy stayed on the steps.

"Ready?" said the man. "Lift!"

He grunted and strained mightily, while the blond boy easily shouldered the upper part. The short man gasped out instructions as they made tight little maneuvers up the steps and finally stood the couch on end to get it through the door.

"Up now! Up a little more! Okay, okay, hold it there. Now lift! Wait, wait! To the right!"

It was in. When they'd set it down, Paula offered some soda.

"Not for me," said the short man. "Thins the blood."

"I'll have some," said the boy.

Paula sent him to the kitchen, while she and the man went over the bill. "I dunno how he does it," said the man softly. "You look at 'im, he's nothin', but he lifts an' it don't bother 'im at all."

"I noticed he took the top end," said Paula.

"Yeah, so?"

"Well, that means you had all the weight, doesn't it?"

The man cocked his head. "You know, you might be right. Son of a gun, I wonder if that could be it." He nodded. "You know what? Next time, I leave 'im out completely. I take a tump line and leave him out. They ask me if I need another man, I tell 'em just give me a tump line."

"He's in there thinning his blood," whispered Paula as she signed the receipt. "He probably hasn't much longer to go, anyway."

197

The next weekend, she put up curtains. "I want to hang some pictures," she told Elliot. "Mr. Horvath said he would give me some special screws, or something."

"What kind?"

"I forgot what he called them . . . uh, let's see. A name. Oh—I donno, Mindy-bolts?"

"You mean mollys?"

"Yeah." She grinned sheepishly.

"No good," said Elliot. "Those are for plasterboard, and these walls are real plaster. You need Jordan anchors. Go to the hardware store and ask for plastic anchors."

"A human encyclopedia," said Lucy, standing nearby.

"And you can pay for me in easy monthly installments," said Elliot.

Paula got her copy of *House and Garden* and held it up, opened to a page showing a picture of a room. "Something's wrong," she said. "Something didn't come out right. What's wrong with it, Elliot?"

Elliot looked at the picture, then back at the room. "Is that what you're trying to make?" He went to a closet, took out a jacket, and slipped it on.

Paula nodded yes.

"Well, for one thing," said Elliot. "It's not on Park Avenue."

He stepped around behind her, wrapped his arms across her waist, and tried to kiss her neck, but she squirmed away.

"We really could use another armchair," she said. "How many more weeks do you have to play before I can have an armchair?"

"Depends," said Elliot.

"On what?"

"On whether you'll take one without arms. If you will, the answer is about a year."

He moved in again, this time kissing her on the lips before she could resist. "Momma Bear has done the cave real nice," he said as he started away.

"Where are you going?" asked Paula.

"I've got to plow the north forty," said Elliot.

"What north forty?"

"Jeez! Put an apron on the girl and she loses her sharpness. I've got a matinee. It's Sunday, remember?"

"Ohh . . ." Paula groaned. "Korvettes is open. I thought you'd help me pick out some lamps."

"Some?"

"All right, one."

"Sorry. How about Lucy? Why not take her?"

A voice called out from the bedroom. "Can't take Lucy. Lucy has homework. Lucy's arm is falling off from writing the same thing hundreds of times."

Elliot shrugged and started for the door. Paula ran after him and flung her arms about his chest. "Hey!"

"Did I do something?" he asked.

"Yes, you did something," she said. "You did a lot of things. I'm crazy about you."

"Oh," said Elliot, cocking his head. "Well, I'm fond of you, too. I think you have some very nice qualities." He reached behind him and opened the door. "Oh, by the way, leave Tuesday morning open."

Paula released her grip. "What are we doing Tuesday morning?"

Elliot raised his eyebrows. "Tuesday is supreme sacrifice day."

"What?"

"I definitely dislike people inserting pointed metal objects under my skin—and, worse, into my conduits—in order to withdraw the sacred and life-giving fluids therein. But I will make an exception because of my high regard for the present company."

"Elliot," said Paula, "I cannot understand you. What are you saying? What are you talking about?"

"Me and you," said Elliot. "Uh, I mean you and me. And I'm talking about blood tests." He went out, closing the door behind him, leaving Paula staring at nothing.

I think he just proposed, she thought, stunned.

Chapter *13*

Elliot was cheerful. The theater had been nearly full, and the skits had gone particularly well, including the improvisations. In the last one, Elliot had pretended to be an aggressive American literary agent trying to sell Solzhenitsyn's *One Day in the Life of Ivan Denisovitch* as a half-hour TV situation comedy. Linda had been the network programming chief.

"It's like *Stalag Seventeen*," Elliot had said, "except these are Russians, not Germans."

"You mean *Hogan's Heroes*," said Linda. "No, I'm sorry, I don't see it. This Solz—whatever—has no track record."

"Look, there's good sketch material here, really. I mean, it snows a lot, and they have to lay bricks, and they eat gruel. There could be a lot of funny eating scenes, because they have to scoop it up with their hands."

"Could the gruel be a soft cereal instead? We wouldn't have to name it, but the Quaker Oatmeal people might be interested if we left one of their packages showing in the background."

"Sure. Great idea! Listen, how about we give you a pilot, okay? Let me speak to Alexandr about it and see what he wants. I'll tell you, he won't ask much."

"Well, all right," said Linda. "If Al wants to do it, let him do it. Is he working on anything right now?"

"Oh, yeah," said Elliot. "A feature comedy about Soviet prison abuses. In fact, I'm already negotiating with two major studios. Al really didn't see the commercial possibilities, but I think I'm finally getting through to him."

"Sounds intriguing," said Linda. "Call me when you've spoken to him, and we'll have lunch."

Backstage, as the cast walked to their cubicles, Elliot caught up with Linda.

"Hey, four stars for that one. That was a definite four-star show."

"Really? You thought so?" said Linda. "I thought I was kinda shitty."

"No, no. Didn't you hear the audience? No, that was one I'd like to bottle."

"I just want to go home and sleep till Wednesday."

Elliot entered his tiny cubicle. It differed from his *Richard III* cubicle by having solid side walls—if you call quarter-inch plastic panels solid—and a pleated maroon curtain for a door, instead of a sheet. Elliot pulled the curtain shut and began to undress. It had been a good day thus far—marriage proposal to Paula in the morning and a successful, invigorating performance in the afternoon. He yelled over the tops of the panels, "Deputy? There's no air in here!"

"You don't need air!" yelled one of the other actors. "You-all is actors!"

"Yes," said Elliott, "but we're also human beings. We are not cattle."

"I think we got a stray cow," said the other voice.

Elliot removed his trousers and stood naked in the cubicle. "Let's hear it for the actors!" he yelled.

A loud cheer went up from the rest of the company. Then a voice spoke directly outside his curtain.

"Hello?"

"Hello," sang Elliot.

"Is anyone in that thing?"

"It depends."

"On what?"

"On who you are. Who are you?"

"I would knock, but I don't know how to knock on a curtain."

"Who *is* that?" said Elliot, wrapping a towel around him and knotting it at the waist. He pulled back the curtain. Staring at him were a very tall, well-dressed, middle-aged man and the most ravishing girl Elliot had ever seen. She was a kind of compact, narrower-boned Sophia Loren, with all the same attributes except that they looked, if possible, even more spectacular when distributed over her smaller frame. Elliot could barely take his eyes off her.

"Hello," said the man, offering a hand, which Elliot shook dazedly. "Name's Oliver Frey."

"Who?"

"Oliver Frey," said the man again slowly. "Is that all right?"

"Oliver Frey, the director?" said Elliot. He thought: I've got to blank out the girl or I won't be able to conduct a conversation.

"I believe so," said Frey.

"No kidding?" said Elliot, trying to get his bearings. "Jesus, it's nice to meet you. Oliver Frey, whaddaya know."

Frey smiled pleasantly.

"Plised to mit you," said the girl. Her voice was thick with foreign accent.

"This is Gretchen," said the director. "It's not possible to pronounce her last name."

"It hass many, many sections," said Gretchen.

"It takes up two lines even when you abbreviate it," said the director. He laughed, and the others chuckled along with him.

"It's okay," said Elliot, and he turned to Gretchen. "How do you do?"

He extended his hand. Too late, he felt the knot begin to move on his waist. The towel slid down around his legs. He gasped and quickly snatched it back. "Whoops! Jesus. Sorry about that."

"Don't worry," said Gretchen. "I was not bort."

"Excuse me?" said Elliot.

"*Bored,*" said Frey. "She said she wasn't bored."

"Oh. Oh, thank you. I mean—well . . ."

"We thought you were wonderful," said Frey.

Elliot envisioned himself diving suddenly into Gretchen's dress, lodging in one of the crevices of her body, and living there for the rest of his life. It simply wasn't fair to construct a woman like that and then have her walk around. Normal females looked like trees by comparison.

"Really?" he said. "Is that what you thought?"

"I have very little reason to lie," said Frey.

"Well, it's a good group," said Elliot.

"I'm sure."

"They're all terrific kids."

"I loved them all," said Frey, "but some better than others. You're very talented, you know."

Elliot feigned embarrassment. "Oh? Well . . ."

"Don't pretend to be embarrassed."

"Okay . . . thanks."

"Well," said Frey, "we don't want to keep you."

"That's all right. I'm in no hurry."

"I did have one question I wanted to ask."

"Ask."

"Would you be interested in a movie?"

Elliot again felt himself reeling. "You mean making one?"

Gretchen tittered.

"Well, we could *go* to one," said Frey, "but I think working is much more fun."

"With *you*?" Elliot knew he should play it cool, but he was far too excited. "Yeah. I'm interested."

"I am, too."

"*Certainly*, I'm interested," said Elliot. "You kidding? Sure." Watch it! he thought. Don't act too hungry, or you'll turn him right off.

"It's not the world's largest part," said Frey, "but I think you'll have fun."

Elliot shrugged, as if to say: Who cares about large parts? Small parts are perfect.

"One possible hitch," said Frey slowly.

Uh-oh, here it comes, thought Elliot. They want me to play Richard the Third dressed in a gorilla outfit. *Richard Goes to Planet of the Apes.* Or else . . . He had a sudden fleeting vision of himself in a porno movie, him and Gretchen. . . .

"If I said you leave tonight, would that be rushing you?"

"Tonight?" echoed Elliot.

"Why don't we leave all that to the business people. Who handles you?"

Elliot grinned, and Frey grinned back.

"I mean your business," the director said.

Elliot kept grinning.

"Request permission to rephrase that, your honor."

205

"Permission granted," said Elliot. "The jury will disregard the previous remark."

"Is there someone I can contact?" said Frey. "An agent? A mother?"

"Toby Richards," said Elliot. "Agent. Six-oh-one Madison. She handles me as a charity case. Like Legal Aid."

"I know Toby very well," said Frey. "Known her for years. Look, I'll get in touch with her soon as I leave here and make the arrangements. Can you speak to her later on?"

"Sure," said Elliot. "Uh, look, there's something I think you should know."

"You have smallpox. Two hours to live."

"Worse," said Elliot. "I've never done a movie. I just want you to be aware of that."

"Honesty is my favorite virtue," said Frey benignly. "You'll be replacing an actor I didn't like."

"I hope you won't be disappointed," said Elliot.

"I won't be," said Frey. "You were really wonderful. It's obvious you know what you're doing. I look forward to seeing you on the Coast. Goodbye."

He extended a hand, and Elliot shook it.

"Uh, right. Yeah. Goodbye." Elliot looked over at Gretchen. "Nice meeting you. Sorry I exposed myself."

"I suppose you want your door closed," said Frey, halfway through the curtain.

Elliot nodded, and Frey pulled it shut after him. Elliot sat down, drained and numb. He looked at himself in the mirror. "That was Oliver Frey," he said aloud. "You're going to be in his movie."

Suddenly, above the tops of the cubicle wall, heads began to appear. Everyone in the cast was watching him.

"Terrific!" said one girl.

"Congratulations."

"One day with us, and he catapults to stardom."

"Take me with you," said Linda. "I'll do anything but clean, cook, or screw."

"Thank you all," said Elliot happily. "And now, for a finale, I am dropping my towel."

"Do something interesting instead," said Linda.

Toby Richards was a bony, crochety, middle-aged woman, and one of the best actors' agents in New York.

"I represent artists," she'd told Elliot when they first met. "You hear that, young man? Artists. There are people who dabble in acting, there are actors, and there are artists. The first two, I don't want. I'm rich beyond your wildest dreams, and shit I don't need. I take on only those people who please me, whether or not it's lucrative. Am I browbeating you?"

"Well . . ."

"Good."

Now Elliot sat in her living room, Toby's huge, silken Persian cat lying on his lap. "I'm sorry to bother you like this on a Sunday," he said.

"What's the bother?" said Toby, inhaling a cigarette. "It's no bother."

"It's just that this guy Frey seemed in a big hurry."

"That's the way he works. He's a maniac; no one can get along with him. But that's lucky for you."

Elliot stroked the cat and sneezed. "What's her name again?"

"Barry," said Toby. "She's a he."

"Very un-catlike name."

"You understand the terms?" said Toby, puffing

207

nervously. "Did he explain them to you? He called here about an hour ago."

"He said I gotta go out to Hollywood tonight. Hey, what about the tickets, by the way?"

"They're holding the tickets at the airport for you," said Toby. "Can you remember? I better write it down."

She stood up, walked to an end table, and began to scribble on a small pad. "And it's not Hollywood, for Chrissake."

"What?" Elliot's heart began to thump. He stroked Barry faster.

Toby turned. "It's not Hollywood, it's Seattle. That's where they're filming. American Airlines flight nine-oh-two. Leaves from Kennedy at eight-forty-five. You got that? It's all here on the paper." She handed him the note, and he put it in his pocket. "Did he tell you anything about salary?"

Elliot shook his head no.

"Well, didn't you ask him? Weren't you curious?"

"I was," said Elliot, "but all I could think of at the time was holding up my towel so that I wouldn't again expose my assorted genitalia to the most beautiful woman I'd ever just met."

"Again? You mean it happened once?"

Elliot nodded, and Toby burst into laughter. "Wonderful! Wonderful! Uh, she must've died. She's been his companion for years, Greta something-or-other, right?"

"Gretchen."

"Don't worry about it. She'll probably slaver over the memory for hours. Oliver's been impotent, you know, practically since I've known him. Told me himself, and we go way back."

Elliot thought that if *he* were impotent, he

208

wouldn't go around telling anyone, least of all actors' agents. Still, perhaps famous producer-directors were different. Perhaps impotence was a sign of character or sensitivity.

"Your salary is two thousand a week," said Toby. "Straight salary, no expenses. I tried to get you an expense account, but he wouldn't go for it. I did get you first-class airfare, though. That's important. It's important for your image. You must always go first class."

Elliot sneezed again. "I think I'm allergic to Barry," he said.

"Your guarantee is four weeks," said Toby. "He must pay you at least for that. Remember, anything beyond that, you tell him to call me. You understand?"

"Yes."

"Because it's a new negotiation, maybe better terms. Maybe then you get an expense account, okay?"

"Fine."

"You need money?"

"I can make it to the airport, I think," said Elliot.

"If you need, call me back here collect," said Toby. "I'll have him advance you some."

"I don't think I need. A chicken bone keeps me alive for a week."

Toby came over and patted his head. "So?"

"So."

"You're excited?"

"No."

"Liar." She kissed him on the cheek. "Good luck with those crazy bastards out there. And remember, you're an artist."

209

Even though it was Sunday, Korvettes was packed, and Paula waited nearly a half-hour for a salesman. Finally, someone came over, a mustachioed man with slicked-back hair. "Yes?"

"I've been looking at a lamp," said Paula, pointing to a very attractive, sculpted, wood-base fixture.

"That's part of a set," said the salesman. "I think . . . yeah, that set is on sale. Ninety-nine dollars."

"Each?"

"No, I told you. The set."

"But can I buy just one? My . . . uh . . . husband just wants me to get one."

"Has he seen the set?"

"Well . . . no."

"Then how could he have a valid opinion?"

"Well—"

"Do *you* like the set?"

"Of course," said Paula, "but—"

"Is the price reasonable?"

"Well, yes, I suppose."

"Then buy it," said the salesman. "Don't let yourself be bullied. You're here, he isn't. He probably couldn't care a fig about lamps anyway."

"You're right," said Paula.

"This is nineteen seventy-seven," said the salesman. "Women are people now. Cash or charge?"

"Cash," said Paula.

"You're doing the right thing," said the salesman.

"I am if he doesn't kill me," said Paula. "Then I'm doing the wrong thing."

She carried the lamps with her on the bus, struggling through the aisle and into the seat, and lugged them for three blocks when she got off. By the time she got home it was late afternoon, and most of the wrapping had torn away. She spotted Lucy outside, seated on the top stair.

"What are you doing out here?" asked Paula. "You didn't lock yourself out again, did you?"

Lucy looked up then, and Paula saw the glazed, hurt expression, and the red eyes.

"Lucy, what is it?"

"At least we didn't get a letter this time," said Lucy.

Chapter 14

Paula, panicky, raced up the steps. The lamps weighed a ton; her chest ached, and her breath came in parched, superheated gasps. She was lightheaded, unable to think. She stumbled on the third floor and nearly fell. By the time she got to her apartment, the world was spinning crazily around her head. She paused for nearly two minutes in the living room, setting down the lamps and getting her bearings, before she walked through the open bedroom door.

Elliot had his duffel bag and suitcase on the bed, nearly packed. He looked up as Paula came in.

"Sending that stuff out to the laundry, I hope," said Paula.

"I got a picture," said Elliot softly.

"What?"

"I got a picture, Paula. I got a movie."

She leaned against the doorway, once again feeling faint. She knew the sensation painfully well—the remote, detached, dreamlike quality, the hallucination that it was happening to someone else.

"Ohhh, shit!" she said finally.

"What are you talking about?" said Elliot. "It's

a terrific picture. Oliver Frey is directing. I have to be in Seattle on location tomorrow morning."

Paula stared stonily ahead.

"Seattle, Washington," said Elliot.

No response.

"Paula!"

"I know where it is," said Paula. "Far away."

"Who cares?" said Elliot. "I'm not walking. They left a first-class ticket at the airport. You hear that—first-class? Each passenger has his own water bed."

Paula looked at the floor.

"It's a four-week job at two thousand a week," said Elliot. "I mean, it's freakin' Oliver Frey! Christ, I forgot to ask what the part was. Can you imagine, I don't even know the part."

"That's wonderful," said Paula, without feeling.

Elliot continued to pile clothes into the suitcase. "I'm not making any comparisons, but who ever heard of Al Pacino before *The Godfather*?"

"I couldn't be happier for you," said Paula.

"Jesus, I am so scared," said Elliot.

"You? Mr. Wonderful Everything?"

"Spend twenty years building up my ego," said Elliot, "and now, when I really need it, it locks itself in the john."

"It'll come back to you," said Paula. "Trust me."

Elliot closed his suitcase and moved toward her. "What's wrong?"

"Nothing."

"Don't tell me nothing. It's written all over your face and in your voice. Paula, it's four weeks' work."

"Fine."

"Four lousy weeks, Paula. That's a week less than five."

"I know."

"No, you *don't* know," shouted Elliot suddenly. "You think you're getting dumped on again, don't you?"

Paula shook her head. "You tell me you'll be back, why shouldn't I believe you?"

"Because if I were you, I wouldn't believe an actor who was packing, either."

Paula crossed to the bed. "Need any help?" She looked at his dresser drawers, all open, all empty. "No, I see you took everything."

"I heard it's freezing up there," said Elliot. "Toby said I should take all my warm clothing."

The tears began to well up in Paula's eyes; any second they would spill over.

"Paula, you know I would take you if I could. But Toby said they were filming way up someplace in the mountains, very rough country. They have wolves up there, not picture-wolves, but real, live, hungry ones with teeth."

"I always get along fine with wolves," said Paula.

Elliot looked at the ceiling and tightened his lips. "Paula, I thought you would be excited. Jumping up and down. I mean, it's what I've worked for my whole life."

Paula looked away.

"Isn't that what a mature relationship is all about?" continued Elliot. "You root for me, and I root for you?"

"I'm rooting," said Paula. "Believe me, I am rooting. It's just that this is my third time as a cheerleader."

Elliot tried to control himself. Understand her viewpoint, he thought. Put this in perspective. Remember what she means to you. "Okay," he said. "Okay, I get the point."

"What point?"

214

"The one you're making with your face. Forget it. I'm not going. It's not worth it."

"Okay."

"It's not worth putting you through four weeks of hell, wondering whether I'm coming back or not. If I got this picture, I can get another one. I'm not going, okay?" He looked at her.

"Okay," said Paula.

"The *hell* I'm not," said Elliot, pounding his fist against the wall. "That's crazy! Why should I do a dumb, stupid thing because you don't trust me? I'm going. You're just gonna have to trust me. Are you gonna trust me, Paula?"

"I'll plan my days around it."

"*Dammit!*" said Elliot. "Dammit to hell! I hate those two guys who walked out of here. I'm the only one who's coming back, and I'm getting all the blame."

Paula nodded. "No, you go, Elliot."

"You want me to go?"

"Yes, I want you to go. If you come back, fine. I'll be right here putting up my wallpaper. And if not, that's okay, too."

Elliot felt a chill rise up his spine.

"I'll miss you," continued Paula, "but I'll survive, Elliot, because I've grown up these last two months. Look at me. I'm all grown up. It was better than spending a summer at camp. I have never felt better or stronger in my life. Somebody is actually walking out that door, and I am not crumbling into a million pieces. Oh, Jesus, it feels good! Goodbye, Elliot."

Elliot felt sick, and frightened.

"Make a nice movie, Elliot," went on Paula. "Have a wonderful career, and if you're ever up for an Academy Award, I swear to God I'll keep my fingers crossed for you."

215

Elliot swallowed and inhaled deeply. "What is there about you that makes a man with a one-forty-seven I.Q. feel like a dribbling idiot?"

"Whatever it is," said Paula, "I thank God for it."

Outside, there was a quick flash of lightning and a booming roll of thunder.

"You're welcome, God," said Paula.

It began to rain; the droplets beat against the windows.

Elliot grabbed his suitcase and duffel bag. "Interesting lesson I've just learned. Falling in love and becoming successful may very well be the worst things that can happen to a man." He reached the doorway and stopped. "If my plane crashes in that storm—"

"God forbid!"

"If my plane crashes, I'm coming back to haunt you. I'll be dragging chains all over this goddam apartment until you're ninety." In the living room, he saw Lucy standing near the couch. He walked to the door. "So long, *kid*!"

In the hall, Elliot turned his head. "See you, *kid*!"

He took a taxi to the airport.

"Fuckin' weather, I'm tellin' ya," said the driver.

"Yeah," said Elliot.

The rain was pouring down furiously.

"Fuckin' roads," said the driver. "I'm tellin' ya."

"Yeah," said Elliot.

"I'm takin' the East Side Drive to the tunnel," said the driver, "the tunnel to the Gowanus, the Gowanus to the Belt, and the belt to Kennedy—that okay wit' you, bub?"

"I'm from Chicago," said Elliot. "I have no idea what you're talking about."

"That's okay," said the driver, "I ain't gonna gyp ya. Hey, you follow politics?"

"A little."

"Fuckin' Carter."

"Yeah."

"Fuckin' energy crisis."

"Uh-huh."

And so it went, all the way to the airport. When he reached Kennedy, Elliot checked in at the American Airlines desk, picked up his first-class ticket, and surrendered his baggage for loading aboard.

"Our departure lounge is right through there," said the clerk, indicating a hallway.

"What's the gate number?" asked Elliot.

"Gate fourteen."

Elliot walked through the hall until he came to the inspection area, a tiny tunnel with detection devices. An alarm went off as he went in.

"Are you carrying any metal, sir?" asked a guard, who had immediately come up to him.

"Nothing that I—a belt buckle," said Elliot. "Would that do it?"

"Could be," said the guard. "Would you mind raising your hands, sir?"

Elliot lifted his arms, and the guard frisked him lightly. "Fillings in the teeth," said Elliot. "Iron in the bloodstream."

"Mmm-hmm," said the guard. "Thank you, sir."

Elliot lowered his arms. "How about a generalized feeling of intense excitement, but with an aura of tragic personal loss? Would that set off the alarm?"

The guard said nothing, and Elliot walked to a couch and sat down. The lounge was packed. Imagine, he thought. A lousy, rainy Sunday night, and half the world is going to Seattle. From force of habit, he began searching for a good-looking girl to sit next to. And that reminded him. Reuben. Reuben, the sailor on the bus. Wasn't he coming from Seattle? Elliot thought back. It was such a short time ago, and yet so much had happened. Found work in *Richard III*, the Golden Barn, the Inventory—and now, for Oliver Frey. Lost work in *Richard III* and the Golden Barn. And nearly got married.

"Attention!" came the voice over the loudspeaker. "American Airlines flight nine-oh-two to Seattle will be delayed approximately fifteen minutes in departure. Attention. American Airlines . . ."

Poor Paula, thought Elliot. He imagined what she must be feeling. Sunday night. Pouring rain. Abandoned. Ditched again. He squirmed in his seat.

After a half-hour had passed, a second announcement was made: because of a delay in the food concessions, the flight would not leave for another two and a half hours. People groaned.

How the hell am I gonna wait here two and a half hours, thought Elliot. He felt intensely lonely and depressed. He left the lounge and walked out into the main lobby. He decided to call Paula and headed for a phone. And then stopped, changed direction, and headed back to the ticket area.

"I want to cash this in," he said, proffering his ticket, "for two second-classes."

"You mean economies?" said the clerk.

"The cheapest," said Elliot, "whatever they're called."

"Staying more than seven days?"

"Yes."

"That'll be another eighty-one dollars and five cents," said the clerk.

Elliot paid him, pocketed the tickets, and walked away from the counter. *Now* he could call Paula.

Or, better yet, he could get her. It was worth the cab fare not to have to sit around the airport. He walked outside to the taxi stand and climbed into a cab. "Seventy-eighth Street, Manhattan," he told the driver.

Paula sat in her robe at the kitchen table, aimlessly stirring a cup of coffee. Lucy appeared in the doorway.

"I can't sleep."

"Give it five minutes," said Paula glumly. "You just got in bed."

"I can predict the future," said Lucy.

"Yeah?" said Paula. "How about predicting mine?"

The phone rang.

"I predict a phone ringing in your life."

Paula let it ring once more, then lifted the receiver. "Hello?"

Elliot stood in the same phone booth from which he'd called that first night in New York. And, as on that night it was pouring furiously. Except this time a taxi waited nearby.

"Get dressed," he said into the phone.

"What?" said Paula.

"Get dressed. You're coming with me."

"Where are you?" said Paula, thrilled at the sound of his voice.

"On the corner. In my old leaky phone booth. The plane is delayed for a least another two hours. I cashed in first class for two economies."

Paula felt her blood race. "What about Lucy?"

"Don't worry about Lucy," said Lucy excitedly.

"Call Donna," said Elliot. "Lucy can stay with her till we get back. Come on, the cab is ticking away your new bedroom set."

"I thought you said I couldn't come with you."

"I'll tell them you're my analyst," said Elliot. "Actors are known to be very high-strung."

"And you really want me to come?"

"Jesus God, you sure love a love scene, don't you? Yes. Yes! I want you to come!"

Paula began to sniffle. "Then . . . it's okay. I dan't have to. Just as long as you asked."

"Paula," said Elliot, his voice rising. "Don't play games with me. My socks are under water."

"You'll have enough to do there without worrying about me," said Paula. "Besides, I have work to do. I'm gonna spend all your money on our apartment." She paused. "But I'm nuts for you."

In the phone booth, Elliot shook his head. "Jesus, I hope I'm calling the right number. Paula, do me a favor."

"Anything, my angel."

"Will you have my guitar restrung? I haven't been sleeping too good lately." He sighed. "Goodbye for now. Call you tomorrow."

"Come and kiss me goodbye," said Paula.

"I'll wave it," Elliot said. "I'll drive by and wave. Here I come!"

He hung up, got back in the cab, and told the driver to drive past their building.

Meanwhile, Lucy was screaming. "He left his guitar! He left his guitar! He *is* coming back!"

Paula rushed into the bedroom to find the instrument. She dragged it to the window and held it outside. "I never doubted it for a minute," she said. The rain beat against her face.

Elliot rolled down the window of the taxi, waved, and yelled something unintelligible.

Paula waved the guitar. "I have it! I have it, sweetheart! Have a safe trip! I love you!"

Elliot motioned her back inside. "Never mind that!" he bellowed. "You're rusting my guitar!"

He rolled up the cab window and reclined in his seat. Forty minutes later, he was back at the airport.

THE BEST OF THE BESTSELLERS
FROM WARNER BOOKS!

FIRE AND ICE by Andrew Tobias   (82-409, $2.25)
The bestselling **Fire And Ice** is a fascinating inside view of Charles Revson, the cosmetics magnate who built the Revlon empire. "The perfect book; a book about a first-class s.o.b. . . . Full of facts and gossip . . . absorbing."—**Wall Street Journal.** 32 pages of photographs.

MY HEART BELONGS by Mary Martin   (89-355, $1.95)
"An effervescent story about a little lady who believes in the magic of make-believe and maintains a childlike enthusiasm, a sparkling joy for life she can barely contain."—**St. Louis Globe.** Almost 100 photos from Mary Martin's private scrapbook.

THE CAMERONS by Robert Crichton   (82-497, $2.25)
The Camerons is the story of the indomitable Maggie Drum, who washes the grime of coal-mining Pitmungo town from her beautiful face and sets out to find a man worthy of fathering her family. It is the story of the big, poor-but-proud Highlander who marries her, gives her seven children, and challenges her with an unyielding spirit of his own.

THE HAMLET WARNING by Leonard Sanders   (89-370, $1.95)
An international terrorist group has built an atom bomb and is using it to blackmail the United States. "A doomsday thriller." —**The New York Times**

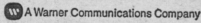 A Warner Communications Company

Please send me the books I have checked.

Enclose check or money order only, no cash please. Plus 35¢ per copy to cover postage and handling. N.Y. State residents add applicable sales tax.

Please allow 2 weeks for delivery.

WARNER BOOKS
P.O. Box 690
New York, N.Y. 10019

Name ....

Address ....

City .... State .... Zip ....

_____ Please send me your free mail order catalog

THE BEST OF THE BESTSELLERS
FROM WARNER BOOKS!

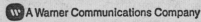